THE REBEL'S REDEMPTION

WOUNDED HEARTS #2

JACQUIE BIGGAR

Cover Design and Interior format by The Killion Group
http://thekilliongroupinc.com

DEDICATION

I have so many people I'd like to thank. First, and foremost my husband, Robert John. Without you I wouldn't have had the courage to pursue my dreams, thank you.

My mom, who has always been my guiding light. Thank you.

To my daughter, Brandy, who teaches me every day to reach for the stars.

To my critique buddies, you know who you are. Without you pushing me to better myself, this book might never have happened.

And to Kim Killion and Jennifer Jakes, for the beautiful cover I'm so proud of, and the formatting and uploading services you provide. Thank you.

OTHER BOOKS AVAILABLE BY JACQUIE BIGGAR

Tidal Falls: Book #1 in The Wounded hearts Series

Nick Kelley spent the last few years of his life working as a dog handler in the U.S. Marine Corps. His sole focus was to keep his team alive in the midst of chaos. When he fails to notice an IED in time and loses most of his teammates, Nick shuts down. It takes meeting and falling in love with a woman in danger to make him realize life's worth living.

Subscribe to My mailing list to find out first about upcoming releases, contests, recipes, and more. **www.JacquieBiggar.com**

CHAPTER ONE

Sergei Barnikov's lips twisted with derision as he followed the manservant who led him through his client's expansive home. This type of grandeur seemed ridiculous to him. The servant, dressed in a flowing white tunic and loose pants, bowed him into a large den where Chenglei sat like a plump sultan amid piles of velvet and satin cushions spread upon the parquet floor.

"Sergei, my friend, what is it that brings you to my humble abode?"

The *poor* home his favored patron spoke of actually comprised of five thousand feet of opulent Chinese décor, filled with priceless silks and antiques. There were enough riches here to keep his family back in Russia in splendor for the rest of their lives. Soon. Soon he could quit playing these stupid games with this durak. A lifetime of effort to reach the status he'd achieved within the organization, only to lose it all, thanks to the American.

"I come with a request. A favor for a favor, if you will." He first toed off his shoes, as was customary, before entering the silk-lined room to sink down onto one of the cushions scattered around a low table set on the tiled floor. He had to stifle the groan crawling up his throat, a legacy of the beatings he'd sustained because of Jared Martin. His bosses were not forgiving of mistakes. They'd already warned him to leave the man alone, but he couldn't. It frustrated him that he had need of the cartel's services, but this was the only way.

"I have a small problem and am in need of your vast resources. In return, I agree to *hold* your money at my casino. We deal?" He strove to keep his expression impassive. One hint of how important this was to him, and the snake sitting across the table would strike.

"Hold on. Not so fast. What is it you ask in return for this most generous offer?" The Mexican-Chinese tone grated on his nerves.

Before he could answer a young woman entered the room; eyes cast downward, a tray of fragrant tea and sweets balanced in her delicate hands. She glided silently over to Chenglei's side of the table, bowed respectfully, and at a signal from him, melted to her knees before setting the china on the round tabletop between them.

"Don't worry, she does not speak the English. She pretty, no? My newest little courtesan. You like?"

Sergei eyed her carefully but could detect no sign she understood them. With her eyes downcast and her head bowed, she appeared like an innocent child. A cherry red dress emphasized her smooth and unblemished skin. It wasn't hard to imagine her in his bed. Her raven's wing hair twisted in a bun behind her left ear, she bent forward to pass him his tea, and his nostrils flared, inhaling the delicate scent of her perfume.

He'd almost dismissed her as one of Chenglei's toys when she sliced him with an upward glance. Topaz, her eyes were that of a tiger. This was no Chinese girl. Upon closer inspection he could see she was tall, too tall for the average Asian woman. He'd heard rumors that Chenglei dealt in human trafficking—here it seemed, was the proof. Something to keep in mind for future business endeavors.

Sergei respected the man; their histories were much the same. Despite his name and ancestry, Chenglei was Mexican by birth. Brought up penniless, he'd joined the Sinaloa Cartel at age ten. A ruthless Sicario, he'd worked his way up to one of the top lieutenants who gave the orders, and reaped the benefits. He'd never looked back. Disassociated himself from his blood kin. The Sinaloa were his new family, and they took care of their own.

These days Chenglei was the head of El León's money laundering enterprise. In charge of millions of dollars made in drug trafficking. His job was to filter those sums through legal companies so it became untraceable. Which was how Sergei came to know him. There was nothing like a little gambling to hide a pile of cash.

"Da, she will do. Have her brought to me later, I sample." Other than a slight tensing of her shoulders, which could simply have been from his rough voice, there was no sign she heard. She finished setting out the pastries, and after a deep bow to Chenglei, rose and withdrew as silently as she'd entered.

Shrugging off his suspicions, he looked to the older man and made him an offer he couldn't refuse. "I have heard of your little problem. I have good answer. You help me, I pat your back, no?"

"You have still to tell me what it is you need from me."

"I wish to find a man. He...owes me. I have searched. He is not in Vegas. I need him found. You help?"

Sergei clenched his fist where it sat on his lap, below the table. He had no wish to let Chenglei know how much this meant to him. The old man was crafty, he hadn't gotten to where he was by being stupid. Sergei would just have to play his cards close to out-fox him.

The Chinese-Mexican sat with fingers steepled, elbows resting on crossed legs and attempted to stare him down, but he would not be cowered by some dirty gang banger, no matter how notorious. His was a greater power—Bratva.

Finally Chenglei leaned back on his pillow and laughed, cutting the thick tension that had pervaded the room. "You are a strong man, my friend. We have a deal. So tell me, who is this oh so important person you cannot find?"

Satisfaction leapt through Sergei's body. Soon he would have his revenge and it would be sweet. He'd been angry and frustrated when he'd found out the man had escaped town, but no more. It had been a gamble to include the cartel in this, but now his path was illuminated. Soon he would return to Russia.

"His name is Jared. Jared Martin."

Jared Martin settled for the night with a heavy sigh of relief. Coming home to face his past bothered him more than he cared to admit. He'd only agreed as a favor to his friend, Nick, who'd wanted to surprise his new fiancé with a vacation. After a harrowing ordeal last spring, Sara's ex-husband was safely behind bars. The two of them needed the time away. They'd managed to find someone to watch her cute kid, Jessica, but the dog had proven to be an issue. Although normally gentle, the retired German shepherd military K-9 could be a handful.

A sorrowful whine woke him from a light doze right before a cold nose jabbed his chest under the blanket. "Are you kidding me? I just put you out an hour ago, mutt." Nick owed him, big time. He cast the downy comforter back and cursed as his feet hit the icy floor. "Come on, pooch, let's get this over with."

He pulled on an old pair of jeans, grabbed his T-shirt, and followed Jake to the door. He could only shake his head over his own stupidity. This is what life had come to, babysitting a diuretic mutt. But then, he'd always been more of a cat person, with their independent nature and 'up yours' attitude. Something like his own.

He sighed and shoved bare feet into a worn pair of sneakers before following the animal out. Jared propped a shoulder against a column on the back porch and let the midnight sky grab his attention. In all the years away, he'd never seen a moon as big and beautiful as it was here in Tidal Falls. If he was being honest, the bright lights and excitement of Las Vegas had paled long before the little mishap with the Golden Key casino a few months ago. Although, when the money poured out of those machines and the sprinklers opened up all over the customers—pure poetry. He only wished he could've been a fly on the wall that day. Some of his best work, for sure. It was their fault. If the Russian and his security henchmen hadn't seen fit to rough him up over a little simple card counting, they could have parted ways amicably.

He wanted nothing more than to put it all behind him, so he'd been happy to help Nick and get out of the city for a while. It was time he came home anyway, eight years was a long time to stay away. Jared stepped off the back deck and crunched through the newly fallen leaves, whistling for Jake. All that answered him was the rasping hiss of an old barn owl disturbed from his perch. Where the hell? He shook his head and started down the sidewalk, hoping he hadn't gotten too far. Jared had already learned Jake had a mind of his own earlier in the day when they'd gone for a walk. They'd started out with Jake practically dancing with excitement, stopping to sniff out every other bush. But when Jared turned north at the end of the block intending to stop by his old friend, Ty Garrett's place, Jake balked and headed off in the opposite direction.

"When Nick gets back, I'm having a little chat with him. Puppy obedience school mean anything to you?"

As they neared the end of the next block he suddenly got an idea of where Jake might be heading in such an all-fired hurry. Sure enough, the dog detoured into the next alley and headed straight for the back door of the Grits and Grace Café. *Damn.* Jared had planned to let his mother know he was back in town. He just hadn't had a chance yet. He could just imagine her surprise. He'd stayed away for years, now here he was back for the second time after only a few months.

The smell of fried onions and bacon had his stomach rumbling. Jake stood at attention, eyes trained on the screen door where they could hear the sizzle and hiss of frying and the faint sounds of the morning crowd waiting to chow down. His tail began wagging a second before the back door slammed back on its hinges and out came his mom's best friend and long-time employee, Susan. She held a large ham bone in one hand while the other reached for a pack of smokes from inside her shirt. "Good morning, Jake. I thought I heard you out here. Look what Grace saved for you, lucky boy." She held it out and the contrary mutt wrapped gentle teeth around the hank and sank to the ground to feast.

Susan caught sight of Jared and let out a squeal he was pretty sure could be heard three states over, before rushing to throw herself into his arms. The remembered scents of coffee, fryer, and smoke from her graying hair made his arms clench her tight.

"Jared Matthew Martin, what in the world are you doing hiding out in back alleys? Does your momma know you're here? She never made a single peep about it. I can't believe you're back in town. You look good, a little thin, but good. Your mom's cooking will fix that soon enough. Well come on, what do you have to say for yourself, cat got your tongue?"

He laughed and tightened his arms around her skinny ribs once more before setting her back to get a good look at her. "How can I get a word in edgewise with you blathering on like that?" He ducked and grinned when she gave him a cuff on the shoulder. She looked just the same, a few more lines at the edges of her eyes, maybe a couple of age spots he didn't recall, but otherwise just the same.

"When are you going to let me take you out on the town, Sue. We'd show 'em how to have a good ol' time."

"You haven't changed a bit, you rascal. Still the handsomest devil I know. Biggest charmer too," she quipped. Her eyes shone with mirth, obviously not buying his blarney. "So really, what are you doing back in our neck of the woods? And why do you have Nick Kelley's dog, Jake?"

Hearing his name, Jake's ears perked and he looked from one to the other of them as if to say, "See, aren't you glad I brought you here?"

Jared explained he was dog-sitting, and gazed enviously as Sue lit one up before offering him the pack.

He shook his head regretfully. "Those things are going to kill you, you know."

She rolled her eyes in reply.

"I just arrived yesterday, and haven't had time yet to call Ma. So no, she wasn't keeping any secrets from you." He leaned a little closer and inhaled as her smoke billowed into the air.

"Well, you'd better go in and see her now. It won't be long before she knows you're here. You know this town." She winked and gave him a little nudge.

Yeah, he did. That was one of the reasons he'd left.

Suddenly Jake stood, his focus back on the screen door of the diner. With a joyful yelp he took off running just as two young children came tumbling out the back door. "Susan," a little tow-headed girl called, "Grace says you better get back in there before she blows a gasket. A big crowd of high school kids just came in."

It was Jessica Sheridan, Sara's daughter. A young boy followed close behind. Jared remembered her from his trip with Frank to Tidal Falls last spring. When they caught sight of Jake, both kids started chattering like a couple of magpies. "Jake, what are you doing here, boy? Look, Chris, it's Jake." Jessica threw her arms around her beloved pet as the boy, Chris, looked on with a wistful smile.

"I see that, silly. Hi, Jake. Hi, boy. How you doing, Jake?" He tentatively held out his hand. Jake gave him a big sloppy lick, and a spontaneous giggle erupted from the kid.

Jared squinted, and took a closer look at the child. That laugh, it sounded familiar, but he couldn't quite place it. He stood a little shorter than Sara's daughter, sturdy with reddish-brown hair and a splatter of freckles across his cheeks and nose. When the kid realized there was someone on the other end of Jake's leash and looked up at him, Jared sucked in a harsh breath. Those eyes. He knew someone with that exact shade of fern green eyes. That giggle...suddenly all the dots connected and his guts tightened up like he'd been sucker-punched.

Annie.

CHAPTER TWO

Annie stood at the back counter over-looking the busy kitchen, and raised her voice above the raucous noise of about twenty teenage kids happy to be out of school early on a Friday afternoon. "Table three needs two fries, a patty-melt on rye, and a house special."

She'd worked off and on at Grits and Grace since she was a teen, and still liked to assist nowadays whenever needed. She'd left Jack's daughter, Tina, who was her own part-time assistant, at The Craft Shack minding the shop while she brought her son, Chris, and his friend, Jessica, here to Grace's for lunch. They'd shared a big plate of Nacho Supreme, and then she'd left the kids enjoying a couple of root beer floats while she watched the front end for Susan to take a break. That's when this crowd arrived.

"Yeah, yeah, tell them to hold their horses. Nicely, of course." Grace warned as she whipped some milk and eggs into froth before dumping a slice of bread in and then slapping it on the sizzling grill. The appetizing aroma of cinnamon, nutmeg and vanilla from the French toast spread through the room.

"Will do, oh master." Annie laughed, tapping two fingers to her brow before grabbing the coffeepot and making a quick trip around the diner filling cups and joking with the regulars. The restaurant was a well-loved meeting ground for Tidal Falls' seniors, her favorite type of customer. They were so cute, the couples wandering in holding hands, the singles talking about bridge club, or dance night. They always had a kind word for her and actively supported her craft store. It was on their recommendation she'd started up her hugely successful knitting and pottery classes.

Annie loved being part of a small community, everyone knowing and caring for each other. It gave her a sense of safety and security. Two things she valued, especially raising a young child on her own. That's probably part of the reason her and Sara, Jessica's mom, had hit it off so well. They'd met a couple of years ago when Sara dropped into the store one day to see if Annie carried any painting supplies. The two women struck up a fast friendship, meeting at the local park on warm afternoons so Chris and Jessica could play together.

When Sara had called last week to ask if Annie would mind keeping Jess so her and Nick could go on a vacation together, she'd been happy to help. From the bit Sara had shared, Annie knew the two of them had been through a traumatic time. And besides, Jess was a doll. It had taken a while but she was finally coming out of her shell and emerging into a happy, playful little girl. Thanks in large part to Nick. He'd shown nothing but kindness and patience with the little girl, which

made him golden as far as Annie and Sara were
concerned. All of which made Annie all the more
grateful for what she had. A beautiful little boy, a
thriving business, and the love and support of the
town she'd grown up in. What more could she ask
for?

She pushed the pang aside, concentrating on
getting her orders out and keeping everyone
happy. She heard Grace asking Chris and Jessica
to run out back and bring Sue in, and was
grateful for the extra set of hands a few moments
later.

"Where'd all these hooligans come from?" Sue
grumbled.

"Their mothers." Grace scowled, looking up
from her position at the hot grill, her face flushed
and sweaty. "Were you smoking again? I thought
you promised me you were going to cut back on
those cancer sticks."

She loved nothing more than to push Sue's
buttons. It often made for some great
entertainment for the customers, but everyone
knew the two were inseparable. Susan was a
mainstay at the cafe. Grace often told her, "You
take a day off, you better be either in the hospital,
or a coffin."

And Susan would answer her back, "Working
for you is going to put me there, you old bat."

She didn't mean it, of course. The two women
were longtime friends and roommates. After
Grace's son, Jared—there was that pang again—
after he left, Sue had gone to stay with Grace for
a while and just never left. It'd worked out well
for both of them. Grace had lost her husband not

long after having Jared, and Susan had never married. They were good company for each other.

A couple of the teens, a gawky girl and a handsome boy, were standing at the jukebox joking over the titles of some of the tracks. Annie remembered being that girl once, wondering why her. Why had the cutest boy in school decided to become her friend—her protector?

He'd been her savior back then, back when she was chunky Campbell and he was Mr. Wonderful. She'd come a long way from those days of feeling so inferior. Jared had helped her grow-up, more than he probably knew.

"Annie...Annie, are you okay?" Suddenly the muted noise and confusion of the busy diner came rushing back—she jumped a little when Jack put a couple of fingers under her chin, lifting her gaze up to his worried one.

"Hey, where'd you go?"

Good question. Why don't you explain to the man you're dating that you were daydreaming about someone else? Why was Jared on her mind so much today? Over the years she'd managed to delegate him to a box she hardly ever opened. A box labeled, The Past. But for some reason today, the lid kept popping open on the memories.

"Sorry, Jack. I don't know where my head is today. When did you come in?" She smiled warmly up at him, hoping to dispel the melancholy she was suddenly feeling.

"Just now, I'm on a break. I dropped by your store but Tina said you'd brought the kids here for lunch, so I thought I'd see if it was too late to join you."

He looked good. He always looked good. His uniform, a perfect foil for his tobacco brown hair, with its tan shirt and pressed black pants. His badge shone from its place over his heart. They'd been dating for a couple of months now. Nothing serious, she wasn't in a hurry, and he'd just been through a nasty divorce, so they were taking their time, getting to know one another. She enjoyed his company, and he was great with Chris. Had even given him a ride in the back of the squad car—it's all he'd talked about for days afterward.

They'd kissed a few times, and she'd enjoyed that too, but had to admit to a feeling of relief that he wasn't pushing for more. You'd have thought she'd be more excited having the town's most eligible bachelor interested in her, and she was—mostly.

There was just this little corner in her heart that kept wishing for the impossible.

"We're finished actually." Then seeing his disappointed look, she added, "But I haven't had my second cup of coffee yet. Our table's right over there by the window. Have a seat and I'll grab us some cups."

"That sounds great. It's been the morning from hell already, and I could use some pretty company." He flashed a tired smile her way before he turned and began to wind his way through the crowded restaurant amid demands of, "Hey, Sheriff, did you get my call?"

"Sheriff, can I have a moment of your time?"

"Sheriff, Betty-Lou let her dog run loose through my garden again. Either you do something, or I will." The last said by old man

Abraham, who lived near Sara's house over on Dearborn Avenue.

Jack stopped at his table and Annie overheard him as she walked by, "Mr. Abraham, now you know you can't go and fill that pup full of buckshot. I told you the last..."

No wonder the poor man looked so tired, he never got a moment's peace around here. Stopping at the pie counter she cut him a big slice of Grace's homemade apple pie, still warm from the oven, piled it up with big balls of creamy vanilla ice cream, grabbed the coffees, and hurried over to their table just as he arrived.

Humor glinted from his warm eyes as he watched her place the heaping plate of sugary goodness in front of him. "You trying to cheer me up, Miss Campbell?" he teased.

"Maybe I am, Mr. Garrett." She flirted back. "You look as if you could use a little cheering up. What happened?" She squeezed in beside him so that they could talk a bit more privately.

"Oh, you know, it's one of those days where Murphy's Law is in full effect. We've been run off our feet since daybreak—this is my first coffee, which tastes mighty fine by the way." His right arm wrapped around her back and settled on her waist as he took a sample of pie—and moaned. "I might have to marry that woman—no offense. This is the best damn pie I've ever had. Thanks in part to the server, of course." His voice lowered, warm enough to melt the ice cream. He smiled, and tempted her with a bite brought up to her lips.

Annie laughed, happy that she had taken some of the shadows out of his eyes. Just then Jessica came sliding up to their table, her short frame vibrating with excitement.

"Miss Campbell, guess what? Jake's here. He was outside when we went to get Susan. How cool is that?"

"That's pretty cool all right. How'd he get here? And where's Chris?" She'd grabbed up a napkin to wipe the ice cream from her lips, when a voice out of the past lifted the hairs on the nape of her neck and sent a shiver down her spine.

"He's here. With me."

The smooth tones rolled over her, and sucked all the air out of the room. Annie stiffened, then crumpled the napkin and slowly turned in her seat—yep, it was Jared all right. And Chris.

Oh.

My.

God.

He looked good. The random thought floated through her mind even as she tried to digest the fact he was finally back. Eight years too late, but he was here. She wanted to grab Chris and run. Run before what was obvious to her became obvious to everyone else. *Shit.*

"Hello, Annie, it's been a long time." Why was he looking at her as if *she'd* betrayed him? She wasn't the one to cut and run without a single word in all this time. Goddamn him.

"Jared. Yes, it has been. A very long time. There were no phones where you were? Your mother probably would've appreciated knowing whether you were dead or alive." Not to mention herself. She'd promised herself she wasn't going down this road, the blame road. It was time to leave.

She turned her back on him, looked into Jack's concerned eyes, and forced herself to smile as if her heart wasn't shattering into a million tiny pieces. "I better get back. Tina needs to take her break. Call me later?"

He gave her waist a warm squeeze, and placed a gentle kiss on her cheek before sliding free. "I'm not sure what's going on, but for what it's worth, I've got your back."

Near tears, she stood from the table, and without looking at either man again, grabbed both children's hands and hustled them out the door.

Jared stood frozen in place, trying to wrap his mind around the fact the poised, self-confident woman who had just slammed past him, was the same sweet girl he'd walked out on all those years ago. She'd looked fantastic, too good for his peace of mind. Especially if what he was beginning to think, was in fact true. *Holy shit.* He could be a father.

Shaky, he looked for a place to sit. The only open spot, her freakin' boyfriend's table. A cop. But beggars couldn't be choosers, and either he sat quick-like, or he was going to be taking up real estate on the floor. He chose the booth.

"Do you mind? They're pretty busy right now. I don't want to be taking up an extra space." The cop could have been a linebacker in his other life. His shoulders took up three quarters of the booth, and he had to be six-three or better. *Great.*

"I know you. Aren't you one of Ty's old school buddies? I seem to remember you hanging at our house back then." The cop gave him his hand across the table. "Jack Garrett, Ty's older brother."

Small towns. Either almost every person you meet is family, or friends of family it seemed. Now that Jared could get a better look he could see the resemblance to Ty. He gave the extended hand a passing glance, feeling inexplicably snarly.

"Yeah well, I'm also an *old* friend of Annie's. I'm happy for her if she's got someone in her life. But you hurt her, and I'll come looking for you, cop or no cop. We clear?"

The sheriff's hand dropped back onto the table, his fork rattling against Grace's fine china. He gave Jared a slow appraisal from glinting eyes. "Well, since we're going the *friendly* route, I'll return the favor. I know all about you too, and I'm not talking about high school. When you and your buddies came to town and raised shit last spring, I made it my business to check all of you out. I've read about your little fiasco in Vegas. You're nothing but trouble, SEAL or no SEAL, so leave Annie alone." He slid out of his seat, threw some cash on the table, and checked his gun holster.

Asshole.

Then he placed both palms down flat on the table so he could get up in Jared's grill. "This is my warning to you. I don't know what was between you and Annie, and I don't much care. But you do anything to upset her now, and I will care. I'll care a lot. *We clear?*" Pushing off from the table, he turned and strode out the door, ignoring the many calls coming his way.

That wasn't the smartest thing he'd ever done, threatening a fricken cop. Like he had any say in what was happening in Annie's life. He's the one who'd walked out on her, his fault, all of it. He was still ashamed for the way he'd ended things that night with her. He'd been a real asshat. Small wonder she didn't have anything to say to him now. She was going to have to though. He needed to hear it from her lips.

"Jared, you're home. Thank the Lord you came back. Give your momma some lovin'." His mom came bustling up the aisle from the kitchen, smiling and crying at the same time and his throat closed right up with affection. He stood and wrapped his arms around her ample frame, lifted her into the air and buried his face in her neck, inhaling all the scents of home. Apples and cinnamon, bacon and eggs, sugar and spice. His momma.

Even after their falling out, he'd known if he ever needed her, she would've been there in a heartbeat. No matter what he'd done, or what he did, she would always be his staunchest supporter. Because that's what family means.

CHAPTER THREE

Annie stomped down the sidewalk, blind to the smiles and waves of the people they passed. Her feelings were bouncing all over the place. *Jared's here. He came home.* She was glad he'd returned for Grace's sake. And worried sick about what she should tell Chris. Or Jared.

What am I going to do?

Anger made her pulse pound against her temples. She should be over it by now, but after seeing him face to face again...yeah, not so much. God, what a mess.

"Slow down, Mom." Chris's laughing voice broke into Annie's discombobulated thoughts. She noticed the drag on her arms as both kids ran to keep up before she pulled them off their feet. A game. They thought it was a game when she'd never felt less like playing in her life.

"Sorry guys, I'm late getting back to work."

You're running, that's what you're doing.

So what? She had absolutely nothing to say to him, or at least nothing he'd want to hear at any rate.

"Who was that guy, Miss Campbell? Why did he have Jake?" Jessica's worried face looked up at her.

Annie knew the little girl still had security issues, thanks to the father she unfortunately shared her genes with. She knelt on the cool sidewalk and pulled both children into a quick hug, as much for their sake as hers.

"It's okay, honey, I know him. He's Miss Grace's son, Jared. I believe Nick and your mom asked him to watch Jake while they went on their trip. You don't have to worry, he's good with animals."

It's people, he has the issues with.

She heard he had a nice reunion with his mom when he was in town for a couple of days last spring, although he hadn't made any effort to get in touch with her. Annie wasn't sure what happened to cause the breach between mother and son, but she did know how much Grace missed her boy.

As they continued down the block, her mind filled with images of the past. At one time they'd been best friends. Buddies. Then one night they'd gone to a party together and ended up overstepping those boundaries. After hours spent in each other's arms, Annie had risen late the following morning, showered, and then spent the time until work singing and daydreaming, impossibly young and happy. Full of possibilities. Until she arrived at the diner to a teary-eyed Grace and a storming mad Susan. It took a while for the story to come out, but the gist of it was Jared had gone home from their night together, told his mother he'd become a Navy SEAL—against her wishes—and after a rip-roaring fight, he'd left, and never came back. Or called. Or even texted. Nothing for all these years.

Jared's father, also a Navy man, had died overseas, which explained Grace's feelings. But there was no justification for Jared cutting them out of his life the way he had. That wasn't the man she thought she loved. It took a while, and a gazillion boxes of tissue, but she got over it. Over him.

When the opportunity came for her to buy into the Craft Shack, she'd taken it. Next month would be their five year anniversary, and she was proud to say business was good. When they arrived at the front doors, she forced her worries aside and stopped for a second to check out how the window display for fall was shaping up. Annie had made a pretty good name for herself with her displays. Word of mouth had people from the city driving to check out her store, which was great for her ego, and good for the town. Yes, the colors popped. The reds, yellows and browns against a background of Ceylon blue, were reminiscent of a Maple forest. They'd draped some of their student's quilting projects over the back of an eclectic old settee Annie had found at the secondhand store. She'd even talked Sara into donating a couple of her paintings; the country scenes were perfect for her imaginary room.

She pushed the glass door inward and ushered the children in first over the tinkle of bells. Tina caught sight of her and waved from over to the left where she was helping a couple of ladies choose shades of wool from an extensive color palette. A trio of teens were looking at all the scrapbooking cutouts, while another girl was over in the corner checking her collection of crochet patterns.

"Okay, guys, I have to get ready for the next class, so can I count on you to behave in the backroom for a while?"

"Sure, Mom. Come on, Jess. Let's go ride our scooters." Chris, ever the little boy, was ready to go burn some energy. With a slight roll of her eyes, Jessica followed. Annie smiled, remembering the days when boys drove her crazy, too. They still did.

She stepped behind the counter, and tucked her purse away before looking over the list of messages Tina had left for her. One from Fiona Radcliffe caught her eye. Sara's friend from Boston with the art gallery, that was interesting. Picking up the store's phone she dialed the long distance number while doodling on the backside of the message—until she realized she was drawing hearts—and flipped the pad over. The phone rang...and rang...and rang. She was just about to give up and try again later when it clicked through and a breathless voice sang out, "Nirvana's, can you hold for a sec? Jim, I told you not to put that thing in there."

Ookay then. Annie smirked. She'd had the pleasure of meeting Fiona last spring when Sara's ex-husband had dragged her to Tidal Falls as a hostage in order to force Sara to hand over the evidence that later put him in jail. Even though she'd been manhandled and tied up, she was still a force to be reckoned with. Sounds as if that hadn't changed at all.

"Hello? Are you still there? Sorry, you know what they say about good help...anyway, this is Fiona Radcliffe." The voice fit the person, vibrant and bubbly.

"Hi, Fiona, this is Annie, Annie Campbell. I have a message that you called?" The teens came up to the till, she smiled and rang them up, gesturing with her free hand to the class list laying out on the counter. A couple of the girls signed up for her beginner's pottery class starting next week.

"Annie, I was hoping you'd call back. I wanted to pitch something to you, and see if you might be interested." She paused a moment and muttered something to the invisible Jim. "A couple of months ago Sara bought me one of your pottery pieces as a birthday gift. I loved it, and showcased it here at Nirvana. I can't tell you how many compliments and offers to purchase I've had." A note of excitement filtered down the line. "So this is it, I want to commission you to do maybe ten or twelve various pieces and set them up here, in Boston. What do you think?"

Holy Moly!

She was dumbfounded. Her heart pounded and her hands grew sweaty. She knew her work was good—it was always in high demand at the store—but an art gallery in Boston? That was big.

"Hey, you still there? Listen, I don't mean to put you on the spot, but I have some serious buyers lined up that are really interested in your work, so it would be beneficial to both of us." Fiona chuckled, as if she could see the stunned look on Annie's face. "I know it's a big decision, with your store and kid and all, so I'll give you a couple of days to mull it over, okay?"

"I don't know quite what to say. I never expected something like this. You're right though, I already have a lot on my plate...I'm not sure. I'll give you a call after I think it over, and Fiona—thanks." Setting the phone into its cradle, she slowly sank onto the stool behind her. This would be an opportunity to put an end to a lot of her financial worries. Sure the store did well, but there was also a never-ending pile of bills that went with it. There was never enough to put anything away for a rainy day. Or Chris's college fund. This could change all that. She just needed a few more hours in a day, not too much to ask, right?

His mother's scent drifted over Jared, warming him in ways he hadn't realized he needed.

"Jared, put me down now before you hurt your back." She laughed, her arms wrapped around his neck like she'd never let go.

Taking the opportunity to give her one last squeeze, he lowered her to the floor.

She seemed shorter—older. Guilt struck, a malevolent hammer to the chest. He'd wasted so many years because of stupid pride. Years he could never recover. Years during which he could have been here, should have been here. Instead his mom was left to manage this place on her own.

And Annie. Annie had a baby. His baby. He knew it, soul deep he knew that little boy was his. Jared had felt a connection as soon as their eyes met. He couldn't even explain it to himself, but he knew. And it hurt. Hurt him in ways that no bullet or knife had ever done. She should have told him. He had a right to know.

"Sit yourself down and we'll get you some food. Susan, bring my boy something to eat. He's too thin." Grace pulled him back to the cop's booth and sat him down as Susan brought him a steaming mug of coffee. Now that he could use.

"I'm not hungry, Ma, I had breakfast this morning, but thanks. Susan, you doll, I love you." He grinned up at her, casting aside his black mood. It was his problem, not theirs. They'd spent enough years worrying about his sorry ass, he wasn't going to give them reason to be concerned ever again.

"You and about twenty others, sugar, get in line," Sue joked and planted a kiss on his cheek, leaving behind a streak of red. She danced off, after giving Grace a warning look.

"That old bat." She used a napkin dipped in his coffee to rub the stain away. "What does she think I'm going to do? Your business is your business, I'm staying out of it. I'm just happy you're home, that visit last spring was too short. You're not doing that again, are you? I need time with you, Jared. I miss my boy." Using the same napkin she wiped moisture from under her eyes.

"No, Mom. I'm home. For good this time." The words tripped off his tongue, and with them, a huge swelling of relief. "Really." The very last thing he ever wanted to do was cause her pain, yet that's all he seemed to do, time after time.

"I'm so glad, honey. I've missed you. We all have." Her eyes, so like his own, filled with tears she didn't bother to hide.

"Momma, don't cry." He reached over and rubbed her wet cheek. "I'm going to go see Ty later, maybe he could use another set of hands. I heard he's fixing the old theatre up, right?"

"He is. Doing a right fine job of it, too. I hope the Fowlers appreciate all his hard work. Where you staying, son?"

"I'm at Nick and Sara's until they come back, then I'll need to find a place. So if you hear of any, let me know."

"Oh, Jared." She grasped his hand in her work calloused one, and he worried at how fine her skin seemed, the blue veins running close to the surface. "You make me so happy. I know things haven't been the best between us, but I want you to know, I've always been proud of you, son. Always. Don't ever doubt that. I love you. I'm selfish enough to want you nearby, but I understood why you had to go. I didn't agree with it—but I understood."

He swallowed hard, blindly staring at the hand wrapped around his much bigger one in comfort and love. Man, what a fool he'd been. He brought it to his mouth for a gentle kiss. Clearing his throat, he looked at the woman who had always been there for him. All the hard feelings he'd carried through the years fell away, leaving him lighter, relieved. They'd still have to talk about it sometime. Just maybe, not right now.

"So, I think I'm hungry after all, how about a piece of pie?"

CHAPTER FOUR

Jared groaned after consuming almost half a deep-dish apple pie. The flaky crust, and cinnamon encrusted baked apples had proven too much to resist. He swallowed the last of his coffee and patted his full stomach on a contented sigh. "Momma, you're still the best cook I know."

"And I always will be." She smiled, and he was relieved to see a becoming blush soften the tired look on her face.

"You need to get some help around here. It's time you and Sue went on some of those vacations you spent so much time planning together." Jared looked around the diner and noticed things he'd missed when he first entered. The walls could use a fresh coat of paint, some of the booths were looking a little worse for wear, and the black and white tile was scuffed on the floors. All the more reason to find a job. He still had some of the cash from his winnings at the Golden Key, but it wasn't enough to do the makeover the restaurant needed.

"As a matter of fact, I placed an ad in the local paper and online. This place is getting to be too much for me." Grace looked down at the table and rubbed at a non-existent spot. "I'm ready for a break."

Shocked, Jared sat back and stared at his mother's bent head. Like Susan, she had threads of gray running through her blond hair that he didn't remember from his visit six months ago. At the time he'd had a little more on his plate, what with his old teammate, Adam, showing up from the dead to help capture Sara's no-good ex. He wasn't sure what to think of this turn of events. The restaurant was part of his childhood. An Anchor. His momma was Grits and Grace. He couldn't imagine one without the other.

"Are you thinking of selling?" Was she ill?

"Oh, no son, nothing like that." She tucked her hand into her lap, and cast a wistful gaze around the now quiet café. "I could never leave this place for long, I'd be lost. Susan and I were just thinking of taking a little break to see some of this country before we're too darn old to go. We figured if we could find a good manager, the place practically runs itself." She looked at him with a little lift of her chin, as if she expected him to argue.

Unaccountably relieved, Jared smiled and reached out to rub her shoulder. "I think that's a great idea, Mom, it's about time. Maybe you'll meet some cute octogenarian along the way." He laughed and ducked when she tried to swat him.

"Get on with you, I'm more interested in when you plan to provide me with some grandchildren, neither one of us is getting any younger, you know," she chided.

Jared searched her face to see if she was trying to tell him something, but couldn't see anything from her innocent gaze. He glanced at his watch and realized he better get a move on if he wanted to catch Ty. "Okay, Momma, I'll work on that and you work on finding a sugar daddy, deal?" He rose, hugged his mom and Sue, and then stepped out the back door to untie Jake from the handle of the garbage bin. It was the only thing heavy enough to keep the beast from getting away. He was still gnawing away on that shank of bone and barely glanced up.

"Come on, mutt, it's time to see a man about a job." Jared hated to go bumming to his friends, but the truth was, since leaving the Navy he'd had a hard time settling down. Everything stateside seemed different, strange almost. He couldn't relax. Even though he'd been out over a year now, he still had trouble sleeping. Women, alcohol, gambling, you name it, he'd tried it, nothing helped. Frank wanted him to see a psychologist, but that wasn't going to happen. He just needed time, everything would straighten out, it had to.

At the end of Main Street, he noticed the double glass doors stood wide open on the old Twilight Theatre. Out front, a garbage bin, its metal lids gaping like hungry jaws, sat half-full of carpet pieces and chunks of wallboard. The building had started to fall into disrepair even before he'd left for the Navy, but he still remembered many a night spent getting hot and heavy in the back row with his girl du jour.

He stepped into the murky gloom. The hammering and sawing in the main part of the building told him where the action was. Jared tightened his grip on Jake's leash. The last thing he needed was the big oaf knocking down a ladder with someone attached to the other end. He bypassed the empty lobby and moved towards the main theatre area, surprised by how large a scale the reno encompassed. There were four men working in the room. Ty was up on stage with one of them carefully removing the heavy burgundy velvet curtains from their moorings. The other two were painstakingly occupied on the filigree up near the roof, working to preserve what they could of the moldings. The seats had already been ripped out and the men's voices echoed in the nearly empty room. Jake let loose a deep reverberating woof, and one of the two near the roof dropped his hammer with an ear-splitting clang as it fell through the scaffolding. Four sets of eyes searched the dim interior until they landed on him and blabbermouth.

Ty raised his hand and hollered, "You the guy the agency sent? You're late."

Jared realized his friend couldn't see him, decided to pull his leg a little, and dropped his voice an octave, "What you expect, man? I don't get out of bed till noon, dude."

Ty hopped off the stage with a poof of swirling dust and marched towards him, riding a wave of pissed off. Jared snickered and the other guys shook their heads and ducked back to work. They knew their boss.

"You can just take your sorry fricken..." Ty was closer now and as soon as he got a good look, his expression changed from psycho boss to teenage glee. "Jared, my God, it's good to see your sorry hide. How many years has it been? Where you been, man?" He ignored Jake's warning growl to grab Jared up in a headlock, the two of them wrestling about the floor for a couple of minutes like kids. "You can't call your old bud once in a while?"

Close up, Jared could see his friend had changed some over the years. His face was harder, leaner. He had lines by the corner of his eyes and mouth, suggesting life might have not been an easy ride for him either. "It's good to see you too, buddy. I meant to stop by last spring when I was in town, but it was a kind of hairy few days, you know?"

"How long are you here? We should get together for a beer or three. We have a lot of catching up to do." Ty grinned his old familiar half smile, as he slapped his cap against his dusty jeans and swiped at a trail of sweat streaking his cheekbone.

"That'd be great. I can see a lot has happened since I left." He gestured to the empty theatre.

"Yeah." Ty looked around the room, tired pride in the set of his shoulders. "You know me, I always wanted to fix this dump up. I'm finally getting the opportunity."

Ever since Jared could remember Ty had gravitated to this cinema hall. They'd spent hours here as kids, then later as teens. If he remembered right, there'd been a certain little blonde who had led Ty on a merry dance back then. He'd have to ask him about that later. For now, he had a more pressing question, "Listen, I'm looking for some work. You in need of anybody?"

"Sure. Actually, that's perfect, 'cause the guy who was supposed to start today, as you may have heard," Ty tapped him on the shoulder, grinning, "was a no show. We're getting into the heavy shit now though, so you'd better eat your Wheaties."

Asshole. Jared had missed this. The kind of camaraderie he'd shared with Frank and the rest of the team. "You just hold up your end, buddy, I can handle mine just fine."

He walked out into the sunshine a short while later, feeling a lot more positive. He looked forward to meeting up with Ty at Duke's after work. It would be good to find out all the news he'd missed around town in the past years.

As he strolled up the street he noticed a couple of familiar faces playing in the town park. Sara's curly haired little girl, Jessica, was riding high on one of the swings, daring the boy, Chris, to beat her. Chris's auburn hair glinted from the sun's rays as he ignored her to dig in the sandbox nearby. Jared jingled the change in his pocket and cleared a suddenly clogged throat. His gaze searched the rest of the park before coming back to the children. He wanted to turn around and head back the way he'd come, but his feet were glued to the cement.

Jake decided to take matters into his own hands. He let out a joyful yelp and bounded across the street, empty of traffic at the moment, thank Christ, yanking Jared into action behind him.

Damn mutt.

Jessica heard him first, and jumped from the swing while still in mid-air, almost causing Jared a heart attack. She landed with an *"oomph"* onto her hands and knees, then jumped up and ran to meet them. Chris, hearing the commotion, looked up and rose to his feet, but hung back, looking uneasy. Jared could relate.

"Jake, hey boy." She giggled as he wrapped himself around her, doing his level best to give her face a much-needed bath. "I miss you too, baby."

Baby? Who's she kidding? Jared checked her over carefully to make sure she hadn't hurt herself. Sara would have his balls in a sling if her girl got hurt on his watch. Then his gaze shifted compulsively to the boy. The kid stared him down, not coming closer, but not backing down either. It was almost as if he dared Jared to do anything to his friend. Jared's heart pinched. Brave little sucker, considering he was all of four foot nothing and maybe forty pounds soaking wet. All attitude, just like his mother. He sported the same rash of freckles across his nose and the tops of his cheeks as she did. And her crazy beautiful eyes. Jared wasn't sure why he felt so certain this little pint-sized version of his old best friend was his, but he was. There was just something familiar about the way the kid held himself, the tilt of his chin maybe, as if ready to take on the world.

The age was about right as well, though he supposed she could have met someone after he left. He suppressed the ugly feeling, and tried what he hoped the kid wouldn't take as a serial killer smile, beckoning him over. "Hey, there. Chris, right?"

Nothing.

Alrighty then. He knew he wasn't exactly Mr. Rogers, but he'd always managed fairly well around kids, at least until now. Jared coughed into his suddenly sweaty hand to clear his throat, and hunkered down to their level. "Not too talkative, huh? That's okay, if I remember right your mom talks enough for the both of you." He'd caught their full attention now, even Jessica had lifted her face out of her dog's fur.

"Yep, I remember being not a lot older than you when we became friends. Whew, that girl could talk the chickens to sleep."

The kids looked at each other and grinned.

"She was a sneaky one, 'cause when you first met her you'd think she was all quiet and shy-like." He stared pointedly at Chris to see if he caught the similarity, "Then boom, lookout, you couldn't get a word in edgeways after she got to know you." Both children giggled.

Truth was, he'd treasured those days. Watching Annie break out of that repressed shell she'd worn and become the vibrant, exciting person he grew to...care about. It'd been worth all the ribbing he'd taken from his friends.

"There you are, I've been searching everywhere. I thought I asked you two to play in the back room. Did I say anything about the park?"

The persnickety voice coming from behind him had Jared's heart skipping a beat in his chest. He actually felt it. *Thump. Thump...thump thump, thump thump.* He noticed the kids didn't look too concerned. Obviously her bark was worse than her bite, which brought up some very interesting images that probably weren't appropriate right now.

He stood, and took a moment to school his features before facing his nemesis.

"Annie."

Annie had run to the park, her heart pounding with fear. She'd gone to the back of the store to check on the kids between classes, only to find the back door cracked open and no one there. Dashing out front, she'd quickly filled Tina in before hurrying out onto the street half expecting to see her kids lying under the tire of some car, squished like a pancake.

Instead what does she find? Jared crouched talking to *her* baby. Making *her* child laugh. He had no right. She wanted him gone. Now. Her hand went to her distressed tummy, trying to settle her nerves.

He looked so good. She'd forgotten just how tall he was, the breadth of his shoulders. His hair glinted in the sun like antique gold, and those Caribbean blue eyes—he wore glasses now—those eyes had always smiled at her, offered her encouragement and support. But they were doing none of that today. Instead they were opaque, hiding his thoughts. But she'd studied his every gesture for so many years, she knew he was angry, furious actually. Well that was fine, because the feeling was more than reciprocated.

"Jared, what are you doing here? Shouldn't you be on your way back to wherever you came from?" Not for all the tea in China would she let on that she knew where he'd been living all these years. She'd made it her business to find out, just in case.

"I hate to disappoint you, my *friend,* but I'm not going anywhere for a while. I just hired on with Ty to fix up our old stomping grounds." Jared waved a tanned hand down the street to the old theatre, "So I guess you'll have to get used to seeing me around."

God, she didn't know if she was more dismayed or excited by the fact he was staying. *Yeah, but for how long?* She'd been down that road with him before. She didn't need a return trip.

"Why? We're getting along just fine. You don't need to worry about your mom. Tess and I take good care of her." She hated the pleading note that had entered her voice, but she wasn't above begging. She didn't want him here. He would just make her life so much more complicated.

"Annie, Annie, Annie, you're going to have these kids thinking we aren't longtime friends. You don't want that, do you?" It was a distinct warning. Either play the game nice or the gloves were coming off.

She looked down at Chris and Jessica, only to see them staring apprehensively at the two adults passing insults like a tennis ball. She sighed and dipped her chin in acknowledgement, before holding her hands out for the kids. Love welled up as she felt their tiny little fingers clasp hers.

"It's okay, guys. Jared and I don't always see eye to eye, that's how it is sometimes. You two argue all the time too, right?" She smiled and squeezed their hands, before turning to the man who had broken her heart. "We have to go. I'm supposed to be teaching a class right now."

They started off down the street, memories of the times her and Jared had spent in this very park bombarding her. Annie couldn't just walk away. Slowing, she glanced over her shoulder to where he was standing alone, watching them leave. "I'm sure we'll see you around sometime," she said, holding up the figurative peace flag.

"You can count on it," he agreed, his gaze a mix of anger and hurt, spearing her in place.

"Bye, mister, I'm glad you were my mommy's friend." Chris's innocent words broke the web. Her gaze locked on Jared's stunned face before she whipped around and hustled the children to the store, her heart feeling bruised as it banged against her ribcage.

CHAPTER FIVE

Still reeling from the afternoon's encounter, Jared drove to Duke's later that night. With a few words the kid had changed everything. He'd gone from an angry, betrayed guy who wanted to rant and rave, to one who just wanted to find a peaceful solution to an age old dilemma. Which of the holidays did he get? Even though only yesterday—talk about getting slammed—he hadn't known anything about any of this, the fact is he did now. He was ninety-nine percent sure he had a son.

He needed a drink.

Jared angle parked and jumped out of his truck. He grabbed a jacket against the fall chill and slammed the door shut behind him. The pulsing beat of heavy bass rattled his eardrums as he nodded at a couple of familiar guys who stood outside smoking. He could see through the dim lighting the bar was packed. Already regretting the impulse that made him agree to meet Ty here, Jared turned to leave when he heard his name shouted from the back corner. Squinting, he made out his buddy's ugly chops, and strode through the crowd toward his table.

His nose scrunched against the cloying mix of perfumes, colognes, and stale beer.

"Hey, I thought you were going to stand me up." Ty said as Jared pulled up a chair and swiped some of the bottles on the table off to one side. Looked as if the party had already begun without him.

"What am I, your girlfriend?" Jared ducked the coaster that flew his way. "I wasn't sure I wanted anyone to see me takin' up with the likes of you."

"You'd be damn lucky to have me, man. I'm a real prize you know." Ty slurred as he slumped in his chair.

Jared wasn't sure what was going on with his friend but it was obvious he was going to need a ride home tonight. And probably a toilet bowl in the near future. Crap. One of the barmaids came wandering by and he held up two fingers. She gave him a flirty smile before strutting some very fine legs over to the bar to fill their order. Too bad he'd lost his interest in a casual hook-up. One glance from a pair of emerald green eyes and Annie Campbell was all he could think about.

While waiting for his beer, he glanced around the room, not surprised by how many people he recognized. It was one of the main reasons he'd stayed away for so long. Living in a small town was like being Mormon, you had a never-ending supply of family all thinking they know what's best for you. He loved them for it, but he'd also felt smothered. And after the final fight with his ma, it'd just been easier to float along a few thousand miles away. He regretted his decision now. Seems as if there were a lot he'd missed with his selfish actions.

A commotion by the front door caught his attention. A big dude stood with his back to Jared talking to the couple of guys he'd seen outside. Their hands waved around as they shouted at the other guy who shook his head back and forth like he couldn't believe he was standing with such idiots. Just then a couple of deputies showed up and in short order, had the loudmouths hustling out the door. Jared had a bad feeling he knew who the hulk was, and when he turned from the door, badge flashing, and a smiling brunette on his arm, Jared swore. Shit, he knew he should have stayed home tonight. Slouching in his chair he scowled as the couple worked their way across the room.

She looked amazing. Her back was to him at the moment, which was good because he needed time to unhinge his jaw from the table. Obviously parenthood suited her. Her once generous curves had slimmed into womanhood, incased in a pair of jeans that lovingly cupped a very fine, heart-shaped ass. A low growl escaped when Mr. Lawman wrapped a brawny arm around her waist, his hand cupped low on her hip. She glanced up at Garrett, and Jared could see her pretty smile lighting up her expressive face.

A tight ache developed in his ribs and he turned away, chair legs screeching on the sticky floor, only to encounter Ty's knowing eyes. Uncomfortable with being caught staring, he searched for a topic that would get his friend's mind on something else. He didn't feel like deflecting a bunch of questions he had no answers for.

"So what got you started in the restoration business? When we were kids you had big plans of becoming the next Dale Earnhardt Jr., or a veterinarian. What happened to that?"

"Well, you know how it is; life tends to get in the way. I found out I actually liked my four wheels to stay on the ground, and I can't stand the sight of blood, so..." He shrugged. "My old man was good with his hands. He taught both of us boys how to respect wood and what it can tell you." He fiddled with his bottle for a couple of moments. "I always did like all those old buildings around town. Thought it was sad when their owners never bothered to fix 'em up, so this is a good fit. Besides, one hero in the family is enough right?" Grabbing up his beer he slugged back the rest of the bottle, slapping it back down with a rattle and wiped a hand across his mouth.

Jared knew all about those kinds of ideals, his father had been a legend in his own family. One that he'd tried, but never quite, lived up to. A sudden wave of energy had the hair on his arms and neck rising. He didn't need to turn to know who had come up behind him.

"Ty, how's it going? I see the theatre's coming along." Jack's deep voice confirmed it.

"Hey, bro, I see you're as popular as ever. Annie, what are you doing with that lowlife? Come run away with me, I'm the fun Garrett, remember?" Ty was back to slurring. Jared wondered how long before he could leave without it looking as if he were running. He inhaled her scent, over the onslaught of spilled beer, perfumes and after-shaves. It reminded him of a spring meadow and a basket full of sweet treats. Annie.

"Ty, how are you? Jared, I didn't think it would be long before you two found each other." Jared could hear the fond memories in her voice and ached to hold her. Apologize. He refused to turn and face her though. He didn't think he could stand to sit there as if it didn't matter while she was with another man. He wasn't that good an actor.

"You need a ride home later? Don't make me pull your keys. Again," Jack said. Ty grimaced at the warning in his brother's tone.

"Don't worry, one night in your drunk tank was enough for me. You should hire an interior decorator, man."

"Yeah, so you made vocally clear. Just make sure you don't become a regular guest and you won't have to worry about it." There was enough worry in Jack's voice that Jared looked a little closer at his buddy.

Sure enough, there were signs Ty had been drinking heavily for a while now. Droopy lines under his eyes, a few faint veins on his nose and ruddy cheeks. He didn't know what was happening with his friend, but he was going to find out.

Glancing back, his eyes ricocheted off Annie's grass green ones to land on the sheriff. "I'll make sure he gets home safe."

Jack stared hard at him for a long moment, and then gave a slight nod before steering Annie to a table near the dance floor. She glanced back at him as they moved away, a thousand things flashing between them before she turned her back, leaving him feeling oddly empty.

"You going to tell me what's going on between you and Martin?" Jack's deep voice rumbled in her ear as he steered her to their table. Annie knew he deserved an explanation; she just wasn't sure what to say. He'd already been married and out of the house when Jared and his brother Ty began hanging out. Jack was eight years older than them, which made him ten years her senior. Not that that mattered to her. He was a handsome, dynamic man, one she enjoyed spending time with. Jack had roots in Tidal Falls, and an important position in the community. He wasn't going anywhere. That made him pretty much perfect in her book.

"There's nothing going on, Jared and I just go way back, that's all. We used to be good friends in high school, and then he left. End of story." Her gaze bounced off his as she searched for a change of topic "It's busy tonight, isn't it? Duke will be happy. Sounds like a pretty good band." Annie's eyes gravitated to Jared's table. "Ty seemed a little under the weather. Is everything okay with him?"

"Yeah, my brother always lands on his feet, he'll be good. He received some bad news a couple of months ago and it's hitting him a little hard, that's all."

"Not his restoration business I hope? I know how hard he's worked to make it successful." She knew just how consuming the fire to prove oneself could become. She wasn't sure what she'd do if her store ever floundered.

"No, nothing like that. One of his old flames who had moved away is getting married in a couple of months, and the wedding is happening here. At the old theatre actually, her parents have owned it for years." He raised a hand in greeting to an elderly couple as they waltzed past on the dance floor.

"Oh, you must mean Katy Fowler. She was a couple years ahead of me in school. I seem to remember her hanging out with the smart kids, right? She moved away to go to university for a lawyer or a surgeon or something, didn't she?" Annie remembered Katy as a fellow geek. They'd done some studying together in the library when Katy's friends weren't around. They'd been your average cool kids, who took far too much enjoyment out of belittling the chunky junior.

"Yep, that's her. She's working toward becoming a cardiac surgeon and met her guy at the hospital. Apparently he was in charge of her ward and they hit it off."

A server stopped by and deposited a couple cold, dewy bottles of beer on their table with a special smile aimed Jack's way. "On the house, Sheriff. Duke says thanks for taking care of the Thomas boys earlier."

Jack lifted his bottle, and tipped it in the direction of the bar where Duke, the owner, stood mixing drinks. The man was built like a tank, larger even than Jack. Bald, his dark skin glowed under the fluorescent lighting. He raised the shaker he held in acknowledgment, bright teeth flashing and muscles bunching under his T-shirt. Annie remembered when he'd shown up at the diner a couple of years ago with his teenage son.

Said he was passing through on his way to California. He heard about the local bar, The Commodore, being up for sale and decided to settle in Tidal Falls. As far as Annie could tell, they were happy here. Duke's son, Ted, helped Annie at the Craft Shack, and frequently watched Chris for her.

Her gaze slid to the back of the bar where Jared and Ty were being served by a woman in a mini skirt and top that left little to the imagination. Jared smiled at something the woman said and a hot flare of envy coursed through Annie's chest and tightened her throat muscles. She should be long past this by now, what was the matter with her?

Taking a sip of her beer, she forced herself to turn away and watch the dancers on the floor. A lively two-step was playing and soon had her tapping her toes and keeping rhythm with her fingers on the edge of the table. She loved to dance, it was one of the reasons she'd agreed to dating Jack. He was like Fred Astaire on the dance floor, surprising for such a large man.

The song ended and before the next began, he had her up and laughing as they joined the others on the wood floor. A west coast swing dance began and he grabbed her wrist and swung her into a series of crazy fast spins before letting her go to out-stretched arms and sliding steps. By the end they were both grinning and short on breath, and bowed to a smattering of applause from the on-lookers. A quick survey of the back corner showed an empty table full of bottles. Jared was gone.

CHAPTER SIX

Jared helped Ty to the passenger seat of his truck, while listening to a drunk singing off-key.

"Meo, mio, let's go party on the bayou."

He slammed the door shut behind his friend, shook his head and looked back towards the entry to the bar. The doors were propped open to allow in the cool night air and let out the stench of overheated bodies and spilled alcohol. Through the crowd he could see figures moving to the country music blaring from tinny speakers. He'd stayed just long enough to watch a few minutes of Annie and the cop's performance, before deciding it was time to take his buddy home.

She was having a blast. His chest tightened. Jared remembered how much she loved to dance. He'd lost count of the numerous times she'd tried to talk him into taking her but he'd always bowed out. The reality was he had two left feet, and pride kept him from admitting it.

He heaved a sigh and climbed into the driver's side, pushing Ty upright before he fed the key into the ignition. Unrolling the electric windows so the air flowed through the cab on the off chance it would sober the idiot up; he backed out of the stall and coasted down the block. Last thing he wanted was any more run-ins with the sheriff's department.

"You know I love you right, buddy?" Ty mumbled from the corner, almost out for the count now. "I loved her too. Why wasn't that good enough for her? Love sucks, Jare."

Ty wasn't going to get any argument from him. Jared knew just how his friend felt. The closest he'd ever come to a perfect relationship had been with his old Navy team. His CO and best friend, Frank Stein, warned him he could only get out of a relationship what he put into it. Jared figured it was easier to count on himself. That way he couldn't get hurt. His mom had always told him he had a problem with holding grudges. She was right. Even as a tow-headed kid he'd hated it when people let him down. When his father never came back, it hurt for a long time. He'd promised he would be home for Jared's eighth birthday. Instead, he'd taken on enemy fire over in Afghanistan and hadn't made it out alive. The little boy had taken it personally, as if he'd stayed away on purpose. The adult version accepted and grieved, but the boy inside of him still wondered what he'd done to drive his father away. No rhyme or reason, it just was.

"Whoa man, pull over. Pull...over."

Shit, catching the green cast to Ty's face and the gagging motions going on over there, Jared slammed on the brakes right in the middle of the street. There was a lot he'd do for his friend but cleaning up after the guy wasn't one of them.

Ty barely got the door unlatched before everything that had gone down, came back up. He let loose with harsh retching noises that had Jared fighting his own gag reflexes. What a homecoming.

"Sorry about that." Ty closed the door and swiped a shaky hand down his pale, sweaty face. "It's been a rough couple of weeks. I guess I thought a few drinks would relieve the stress, you know."

Jared let out a pent-up sigh. "Yeah, I've had a few too many of those kind of days myself. No problem, buddy. Let's get you home and into bed. Tomorrow's going to come way too soon." He put the truck back into drive and finished the couple of blocks to Ty's rancher style house. He'd bought it not long before Jared's visit to town last spring, and had already done extensive renovations to the exterior, updating the outdated wood for a handsome stone siding. From what Jared could see in his headlights as they swept the front lawn when he pulled into the driveway, the yard now looked manicured and immaculate. A big difference from the rundown place it'd been when Ty bought it.

"Thanks, pal, I won't forget this. Catch you in the morning."

"You need a hand getting inside? Wouldn't look too good for the neighbors to find you crashed out on your front lawn." He eyed Ty as he carefully opened his door and sort of slid out, holding the frame for support.

"Yeah, I'm good. No worries. Night."

Jared winced, as Ty slammed his door with enough gusto to push it through to the other side. He made sure his friend made it inside safely, and then drove home through the now deserted streets. About as different from Vegas as if he'd landed on the moon. That was a fairly accurate description of how he'd felt for the past few months. Almost as if he were in some kind of weird bubble where he could see, but not feel much of anything. Except anger, there was plenty of that bottled up inside. He tried to keep a lid on it, but every once in a while—like the incident with the casino—it crept out. Frank was probably right; he should talk to a squint. It just went against the grain to go pouring out his messed up thoughts to anyone. That was one of the first things ground into them at boot camp, no matter what keep your damn mouth shut.

He wheeled around the corner and pulled up at Nick and Sara's house. They'd bought it from Sara's neighbor and landlady, Tess Garrett, Ty's aunt. Nick had settled into family life with both feet, it seemed. Jared was glad for his friend. He'd been through hell and back and deserved a happy ending.

The wind had picked up a bit and was whistling through the bare branches of the Cherry tree in the front yard. Maybe tomorrow he'd do some raking after work. The leaves were starting to pile up. Briefly he thought of inviting Chris and Jessica over to play in them, a favored game when he was a child. Jared wanted to get to know his son. But first he had to have that all-important discussion with Annie. He sincerely hoped she wouldn't try denying the obvious. He didn't want to force the issue, but there were tests to prove parentage. If he'd known sooner...it didn't matter, what was done, was done. Things would have to change now though. Bone-tired,

Jared climbed the stairs and let himself in amid wild barking.

"Shh, you're going to wake up the whole neighborhood." Jake stood guard in the entryway, hackles raised and deep-throated growls that lifted the hair on Jared's arms. Freaking mutt. "C'mon, Jake, it's only me. Behave or I won't get you a treat." The magic word, Jake instantly became his best friend, whining and dancing little circles of glee. The turncoat. Jared grabbed his treat from the cupboard, threw it down, and paced the hall to the guestroom. Done up in a dark blue with white edging, the room was quiet and restful. He undressed had a quick shower and slid beneath the covers, glad the day was done. Or so he'd thought, until the damn dog decided he needed out every fifteen minutes. Sleep was over-rated anyway, right?

Now here he was, wandering a dark street in the middle of the freaking night, looking for a mutt that didn't even belong to him. "Jake, where are you, you flea-bitten-sack-of-garbage-eating-fur on four feet?" Seriously, did he have loser written on his forehead, or what?

Thing was he knew there was a little person who was counting on him to care for her dog until her parents came home and he couldn't let her down. So even though bed was calling his name, Jared continued down the street whistling for a dog with no known manners whatsoever.

Annie looked at the glowing face of her watch and saw it was nearly midnight when Jack pulled up in front of her duplex. She could see the flicker of the television through the thin curtains in the sitting room. Tina, waiting on her father's arrival.

"I had a fun time tonight. It was good to get out and blow off some steam." Jack's deep voice penetrated the bubble of her thoughts.

She heard the intimate tone and braced herself.

And what does that tell you? It told her that she needed to get out more, that's what it told her. As his brawny arms wrapped around her, she forced herself to relax and lean into him. This was Jack. She'd known him half her life. And it wasn't the first time they'd kissed, for Pete's sake.

Her hands flattened against the thick wall of his chest. She leaned forward as his head slowly lowered and…there was a knock on the passenger side window.

Annie jerked backwards, but not before bonking her nose on his chin. And there they sat, her cradling her nose, him rubbing his chin, and Jared leaning down from outside to stare through the closed glass. Lovely, the three stooges.

"What the hell does he want?" Jack growled, his voice shouting frustrated male.

"How should I know? I didn't ask him here." Annie laughed, finding humor in the situation now she'd had time to calm her galloping heart.

The window beside her slid down with a slight whoosh. Grateful for the bracing air she sent a quick sidelong look at Jack's still grim visage, before turning to Jared. "What are you trying to do, scare us half to death?"

His glinting teeth reminded her of the bedtime story she'd read to Chris, *Red Riding Hood*. "Aren't you too old to be necking in the backseat?"

"We aren't in the...never mind. What are you doing here, Jared?" Indignant now, and a slight bit embarrassed, Annie's temper flared. He had no right questioning her about anything, much less if she was *necking*, as he put it. She hadn't realized her leg had started jiggling until Jack's warm hand settled on her thigh.

Jared's eyes flared red.

He scowled at the hand, "I'm looking for Nick's beast. Have you seen him?"

"Jake? Jake's missing? Oh no, we have to find him. Jessica loves that dog." Annie realized a split-second after she said it that she'd essentially put an end to her date. Jack's hand flexed, and then slowly released her leg as he shifted over in his seat.

"Yeah, I better get home. I've got another long one coming up tomorrow. Send Tina out, will you?" He gripped the steering wheel in one hand and leaned over to start the engine with the other.

Annie placed her fingers on his forearm so he'd look at her, a silent apology in her gaze. "I had a nice time tonight, Jack. I'm sorry about this, but you know how attached Jess is to that dog, especially after last spring. I can't just let him wonder around and maybe get hurt. Please understand."

Jack frowned over her head at Jared for a long moment before turning resigned brown eyes to her. "Believe me, I get it. I wish it hadn't ended this way, that's all."

She didn't like the final tone in his voice but before she had time to question it, Tina came running out of the house, all coltish legs. She opened the back door and slid in, sending a curious glance at Jared on her way by.

Jack shot him a hard look before smiling back at his girl, "Hey, peanut, no trouble tonight?"

"No way, Dad, Chris is always a sweetie, and Jess was no trouble at all. We played games, watched a movie, and then I tucked them into bed. Easy, peasey."

"Thanks for watching them, Tina; it was good to get out for a change. Your father is pretty amazing on the dance floor you know." She smiled over her shoulder at the teenager, and then gave Jack one last squeeze before climbing out of the car to stand beside Jared. She tried to ignore his solid presence as she leaned through the window to thank Tina again and say goodnight to Jack, watching as he drew away into the night.

"Okay, so now that you've managed to ruin my date, where did you see Jake last?" Annie hated that her foolish heart so easily betrayed her, pumping blood to her cheeks in a show-and-tell she was helpless to hide. Hoping he would think it was the fall coolness she shoved her hands into her coat pockets and lifted her chin. She refused to let him know he got to her.

Jared turned from watching Jack drive off to give her the big brother speech, "Do you know what you're doing there? That guy has family written all over him."

She huffed out a frustrated breath, "Not that it's any business of yours, but what makes you think that's a bad thing? Maybe I'm tired of going it alone. Maybe I want a man in my bed, and maybe that man might even be Jack." Turning away from his all-too-knowing gaze, Annie searched the neighboring yards for a moving shadow. "It doesn't matter what you think, I just want to find Jake and go home. I don't like leaving the kids alone, even if they are asleep."

Jared looked momentarily flummoxed.

Not surprising for someone who only thinks of himself. Annie hated the cynical thought. What happened to them? They'd been best friends. Now, it seemed all they could manage was to snipe at each other like a couple of Bantam roosters fighting over turf.

She sighed, "Okay, let's start this conversation over. I'm sorry Jake's missing. What can I do to help?"

"Look, Annie..." Jared ran a tired hand through his wavy hair and her palm tingled in response.

She clenched her hand shut and turned away from temptation. Bringing two fingers to her lips she let go with a loud wolf whistle, hoping it didn't wake the kids. She turned back to see a lopsided smile appear, along with an easing of tension across those thick shoulders.

"I'd forgotten how good you were at that. Remember bugging the hell out of Ty and me until we taught you how?" He moved in closer, his shadow merging with hers on the walkway.

She remembered a lot of things. Dangerous things. "Yeah, I also remember how you guys always tried to set me up on dates with your loser friends. That one never worked."

"Maybe we made sure it never worked, you ever think of that?" Jared said half under his breath, before turning away at the sound of rattling bushes not far off. "Either that's the mutt now, or there's a moose in that yard."

Annie was still trying to figure out what he'd meant by his comment when Jake rambled onto the road, as if he had all night and they were idiots for standing there in the cold. Maybe he wasn't far off.

"Jake, you big goofball, where have you been? Get your hairy butt over here. Next time you're on your own, got it?" Jared said as he latched the leash he'd been carrying onto the runaway before patting the big head.

"I'm glad we found him, I wouldn't have liked to tell Jessica her dog was missing. Have you heard anything from Sara and Nick?" Jared shook his head. "Well, I'm glad he finally talked her into taking that vacation."

"Yeah, me too, they deserved a break." He agreed. "Her ex isn't going anywhere for a long time, they're safe now." And they were. Thanks to the combined efforts of the DEA and the FBI, Sara's ex-husband, a dirty lawyer working for the Sinaloa Cartel, had been caught and arrested right here in Tidal Falls last spring. Annie was happy for Sara, who'd managed to find her happy ever after in the middle of all that chaos. Just goes to show, if it's meant to be, it happens. Or not. She looked at Jared crouched down rubbing Jake's furry ears.

"Well, we'd better be going. I'm starting a new job tomorrow and wouldn't mind getting a couple hours sleep," he said.

Annie bit down on the invitation to come in for a moment.

That would be the height of stupidity. Of course she knew it, just like she knew Jack was a much better bet in the romance department. Unfortunately her traitorous heart hadn't received the memo.

"Would you like to come in and warm up for a bit? I make a mean hot chocolate, or so I've been told," she asked, even as she kicked her own butt for doing so.

Jared came to his feet and she sensed his refusal before he even said a thing. The whole embarrassed, timid sense of being just not quite good enough threatened to swallow her up. Why did she invite rejection? She wasn't a masochist; at least she didn't think she was.

"You know what, it doesn't matter." She had a good life. She definitely didn't need to put herself through all the drama that was Jared Martin. "Let's forget I asked that, okay? We've both had a long day; maybe we should just call it a night." She'd already turned away to move up the walk, when she thought she heard his low voice.

"What if I can't forget, Annie? What then?"

She continued up the sidewalk, not allowing herself even a single moment's hesitation to break her stride.

CHAPTER SEVEN

Annie woke late and had to scramble to get the kids off to school. In the chaos of throwing together breakfast, lunches, and sorting homework piles for their backpacks, she missed getting her coffee, which didn't bode well for the rest of the day.

She arrived at the Craft Shack ten minutes late for a delivery and had to apologize profusely to the disgruntled driver waiting to unload her supplies. She was in the process of going over the invoices when the phone rang. Shrugging off his heavy sigh, Annie tripped over packing materials and boxes, making it to the front just in time for the blasted thing to quit.

She returned to the back room, signed the invoices, and let the poor man out the door. Opening her parcels she was happy to see the new potter's wheel, ordered for a class she'd thought of running this winter. There was also a nice variety of wool for the knitting club. And paint for her resident artist and best friend, Sara Reed.

Annie missed Sara, even though she'd only been gone a few days. The two of them had bonded in the last couple of years and she could use a confidant about now. The situation with Jared had left her reeling.

The shrill tone of the phone in the quiet store made her jump. She shook her head and hurried to answer it—she really needed to quit reading thrillers just before bed. "Hello, The Craft Shack, how may I help you?"

Heavy breathing, then an ominous silence.

"Hello?" Still nothing, and for some reason a chill of ghostly fingers tiptoed up and down her spine as the phone stuck to her suddenly clammy palm. "Who is this? What do you want?" Her eyes darted to the locked door as her butt hit the stool behind her.

"Look, this isn't funny. Either say something, or I'm hanging up." It was probably kids playing pranks. She had a sudden vision of herself in one of those Friday night horror flicks. The one where you just know if she opens the door, *she'll be sorry*. And for God's sake, stay out of the shower! A nervous little snicker erupted and she slammed a hand to her mouth to force it back.

She'd just pulled the phone away from her ear when there was muffled laughter on the other end, followed by a faint squawk, "Nick, let me have the phone. She's going to hang up on us, you big ape. Nick..." followed by more laughter and something that sounded a lot like goldfish coming up for air. Ah, true love.

"Okay, you two, cut it out." Annie smiled in undeniable relief, now that she knew Freddie wasn't on the other end of the line. "You can do that later. Nick, hand the phone to my bestie like a good boy now. I was just thinking about you guys. I told you I was telepathic."

"Or just pathetic." Nick got in a parting shot as Sara took over the phone.

"Ignore him, he's a tease. How's my baby? I miss her so much. I miss everyone."

"Never mind, you're not allowed home for another week and a half yet. Do I need to have a talk with your man? Maybe he needs some lessons in the art of seduction?" Annie grinned as she heard his growl in the background. Mission accomplished. There was nothing she enjoyed more than needling Nickolaus. "Jessica is doing fine. She and Chris are having a blast together."

"Can I talk to her for a minute? I want to tell her about seeing the orcas, she loves *Free Willy.*"

"You're too late, I took them to school a little while ago. Don't worry, Mom, you just work on providing her with the brother or sister she requested for her birthday."

Sara giggled like a teenager. Annie was happy for her friend, even as her own heart gave a little pinch of envy. Shrugging it off, she grinned into the empty room. "Hey, I had to try. I make a great aunty, you know."

"You do, you're the best. Thanks for doing this for us. Nick and I are so grateful. We're having a wonderful time here, it's gorgeous. We've been whale watching, touring, and yesterday we went to Butchart Gardens. I'm getting a ton of new ideas for paintings. Get ready to sell me a pile of supplies."

"Funny you should mention that, I was just unpacking a new shipment and there are a few paints in there I think you'll love."

"Ooh, I can't wait." Then in a fainter voice, "I'm having a great time, Nick. No, I'm not ready to leave yet, don't be silly." Sara came back on line. "Men. You say one thing and they think you mean something totally different. Have you seen Jake around? Nick's friend, Jared, is looking after him. I hope he's not having too much trouble."

Now she tells me. It would have been great to have a heads-up a little sooner so she could have prepared herself. As much as she could, anyway.

"Yeah, the kids and I saw them yesterday. Jake looks good, Jessica was sure happy to see him."

"And Jared? Pretty hot, isn't he?" Sara teased, and Annie could practically hear the matchmaking wheels turning.

Seeking an end to that road before her friend started down it, she hastened to remind her of her recent date. "Yeah, hot. Speaking of which, Jack and I went out dancing last night. I think we could be getting serious."

"Oh really? Well, that's great. I'm happy you're finally getting out there. You needed to forget the past and find someone, Annie. Take it from one who knows, it's worth it."

More murmuring and smooching sounds. Annie decided to sign off before her poor ears were permanently ruined. "Yeah, I agree. It's time, past time actually. I better get back to work, you kids have fun, and yes, I'll hug Jessica for you. Bye, miss you."

"I'll call back when she's home next time. Bye, miss you too. See you in a couple of weeks." Click went the phone. Annie held on to the lonely sound of the dial tone for a couple extra seconds before shutting things down on her end. They sounded happy. She was glad for them, she really was. But it highlighted the fact her and Chris were alone.

Annie hadn't seen her own father in years. Just as well really, she'd never lived up to his expectations anyway. Especially after she'd gotten herself pregnant. He'd walked out on their little family without ever having met his only grandson and never returned. Her mother, not a strong person to begin with, sank into a deep depression helped out by alcohol and pills. A couple of years later, she'd given up and passed away, leaving Annie alone with her baby and a mountain of bills.

Thank God for Grace, who'd stepped in, offered her a job and a room to rent. Annie always wondered if she'd known about her and Jared, but was never brave enough to ask. She wasn't sure what would have happened if Grace and her friend Tess, Jack's mom, hadn't been there to help a scared and lonely teen. She owed them a lot. Which is how she'd wound up on a date with Tidal Falls' Chief of Police a couple of months ago. Annie had known Jack for years. As a teen she'd even had a crush on the handsome high school football star. Until Jared.

Done with feeling sorry for herself, Annie slid off the stool and went back to work on unpacking her new freight. There were some nice carving knives packed in one of the boxes. She'd been trying to come up with ideas to tap into the male clientele in the area. It was proving to be slow going, though. Not very many guys wanted to get caught entering a craft store, like it emasculated them or something. A mental image popped into her head of a man throwing on a wig and a dress in order to sneak inside, long hairy legs encased in nylons and high heels. She chuckled at the crazy picture, and hefted the box to carry it out front. As she moved through the doorway, a shadowy figure detached itself from the wall. She screamed and her arms jerked into the air, sending knives flying everywhere.

CHAPTER EIGHT

Jared drove his truck into the theatre's gravel lot and parked next to Ty's pick-up. He looked forward to some physical labor in order to get his mind off Annie and her son. He grabbed his jean jacket against the chill of the morning, hopped down out of his four-by-four and strode up the stairs to the front door. The noise of circular saws mixed with the pounding of hammers and air guns, creating a symphony of sound. Jared felt his shoulders loosen, the stress bleeding out of him at the familiar scent of fresh-cut wood and paint. Though his natural skill lay in electronics, he'd always enjoyed the physicality of the construction business.

A couple of men, dressed in the standard garb of T-shirts tucked into loose jeans, steel-toed work boots and hard hats, were lifting the counter off the old concession booth and looked up as he entered.

"Boss around?" he asked.

"Not yet," one of them answered, his biceps flexing with the weight of the stand.

Jared nodded his thanks and moved out of their way as they hauled it out the door. Now what? He didn't want to just leave. He'd told Ty last nigh...shit, that's it. The bugger undoubtedly had the hangover to beat all hangovers. No wonder his truck was sitting outside. He'd probably known he was going to tie one on, and had planned on cabbing it home. Instead, Jared drew the short straw. Well, he might as well start earning his wage, and see if the boss needed a ride to work.

He palmed his keys out of his pocket and followed the men back into the sunshine. They'd set up a couple of sawhorses and had the old countertop laid on top. The guy who'd answered him earlier was plugging in a planer. Jared liked the fact they were preserving the integrity of the old building by re-using whatever they could.

He gave the men a short nod and headed to his pickup. It wasn't the easiest on fuel that he'd ever driven, but man, when that diesel engine fired and rumbled up through the seat of his pants, he felt like giving the old Tim the Tool-man, "*argh, argh, argh.*" Power. Man's best friend. He shifted into gear and trolled up Main Street. His foot eased up on the pedal as he neared the Craft Shack, but all he could see was some kind of fall display blocking his view into the store. He didn't like how things had ended last night with him and Annie. It wouldn't have hurt him to go in and have a cup of flipping cocoa, would it? Except yeah, he'd been afraid it would.

There'd been a time when he would have cheered at the thought of spending a couple of late night hours in Annie Campbell's company, but that was before he'd screwed up their friendship forever. And now he might have a child to consider.

He stomped down on the gas pedal as if he could outrace the guilt and remorse following him like a black cloud. Why hadn't he ever asked about Annie over the years? Contrary to what she believed he had called his mom on birthdays and holidays. Short, awkward, stilted conversations where each of them worked to maintain the peace. He had no such excuse for Annie. They'd been best friends and he'd repaid that by treating her like a cheap lay.

He drove around the corner and down the twelve blocks to Ty's street. His mood lightened when he caught sight of a lone figure trudging through the old school grounds. This was going to be fun.

Jared waited at the end of the block for Ty to hit the sidewalk and then idled behind him. He was about to blast his horn when Ty shot him an annoyed look over his shoulder. Jared snickered and crawled up, lowering his passenger window. "How's the head?"

"Ducky. Aren't you supposed to be at work?" Ty kept his gaze trained straight ahead, as if turning too fast might have dire consequences, which going by last night's events, might well be true.

"Yeah, well, I went there bright and early, just like the boss-man said, but there was no one there to tell me what to do, so I left."

"I can tell you what to do," Ty growled. "You here to give me a ride, or just chat it up?"

Jared laughed and pulled ahead a couple feet to let his friend in. He'd never been a drinker, and was extra glad of that fact as he watched Ty climb into the cab like an old man. There was nothing like a bottle of booze or a woman to bring a man to his knees. Jared gunned the gas, and earned a sharp curse from the other side of the cab where Ty had been trying to buckle up.

"Watch it; you just about spilled my coffee."

"Someone got out on the wrong side of bed this morning, or did you even make it to a bed?" Jared smirked.

"Two words." Ty leaned his head against the cool glass and sighed. "You're fired."

Jared leaned forward and turned on the stereo. Loud.

Annie's heart tried to leap out of her chest, one hand muffling her scream, while the other clutched the now half-empty box. Why hadn't she made sure she locked the door behind the delivery guy this morning? Of all the asinine, irresponsible things to do

"I...I'm sorry, we're closed right now. Can you ma...maybe come back later?"

Like never.

The stranger—she was pretty sure she'd never seen him before—stayed to the shadows, denying her a clear view of his features. He wore an old-fashioned bowler hat tipped forward over his eyes, and a black greatcoat, one hand tucked into the pocket. She was probably about to star in her own horror flick. *Killed with her own merchandise.* She could see the headlines already. Annie kept a nervous gaze on that pocket, her imagination going into overdrive.

When the silence threatened to explode in her head, he bent and picked up one of the carving knives she'd graciously sent his way. His thumb skimmed up and down the blade. She didn't think she'd ever been so scared in her life.

"Please, I have no money. What do you want?"

That got a reaction. His hand stilled on the blade and piercing eyes looked up and pinned her in place. "Tell Martin I here. There is nowhere he can hide." He threw the knife. Annie gasped and recoiled as the blade flew through the air and embedded itself obscenely in the heart of her sewing mannequin. "Tell him he must pay." Without another word, he disappeared out the door, a dark wraith.

Annie sank to the floor in a boneless heap. Now that it was over her teeth chattered, and shivers racked her frame. Who was he? What did he want? She wanted to believe it was all a misunderstanding and he'd come to the wrong door, but in her heart she knew better.

This was about Jared.

Jared spent the morning working outside with the men to build some new boxes for the theatre's speakers. They'd also finished sanding the concession counter, which had turned out to be a beautiful walnut under all the multiple layers of chipped paint.

Now he made his way through the narrow hall leading into the main theatre. The room looked much the same as it had on his first visit. With the carpets lifted, the original hardwood flooring gave character to the space. The men had stripped the stained wallpaper from the walls, and were replacing it with vintage paper in an antique gold overlaid with embossed red velvet, echoing the filigree work on the ceiling. As Jared got closer he overheard Ty arguing with someone about the lighting.

"I don't see how I'm supposed to get this finished in the timeframe you're asking for. It can't be done." Ray, or at least that's what his nametag said, slapped his palm over the schematics laid out on top of the stage.

"Then find a way. I'm on a tight schedule. When I hired you, you said it wouldn't be a problem." Ty shot Jared a frustrated glance and jammed his glasses up his nose.

"Yeah well, that was before you decided to wire in the Radio City Music Hall. What the fuck, man, this is small-town U.S.A. What are you trying to prove?" Ray yanked his cap off his balding head, grabbed a wrinkled cloth from his back pocket, and wiped the sweat from his brow.

Jared decided it was a good time to step between the combatants. "Mind if I take a look at that?" He pointed his chin at the plans.

"Knock yourself out. I quit." Ray threw a disgusted glance around the room, then stomped towards the exit, his round body swaying from side to side.

Ty threw his hands into the air. "Now what am I going to do? He was the best electrician available. I'm screwed."

Jared turned his attention to the diagrams. While elaborate, it wasn't impossible. "Whose idea was this?"

"Mine, why?"

"No reason, they're pretty good, that's all."

"I went to a planner in Seattle. Explained what I was looking for, and they did up the sketches. I need to do this, Jared." Quiet desperation tinged Ty's voice, betraying how important this was to him. He was still in love with his old girlfriend, Katy. This would be his final gift to her.

"I'll do it." Jared said abruptly.

"What?"

"I said I'll do it. Can't have you crying all over the place. Ray took his rag with him, there's nothing to wipe up your crocodile tears." Jared kept his eyes on the drawings to give his friend a moment to regain his composure.

The four amigos. As teens they'd done everything together. But when Katy's parents found out she was serious about *"that Garrett boy,"* the trouble began.

To be fair, Katy was a sweet kid. She'd only wanted to please her parents. Parents who always managed to find fault with anything she or her twin, Kyle, did. Jared could remember more than once when he and Annie would be hanging out, and she'd receive a call from Katy looking for a sympathetic ear. Finally, Ty couldn't take the pressure anymore and they had a big blowout. She ended up going to graduation with Tony Randolph, a guy her parents approved of. It was the beginning of the end for them. She moved away to California, and he never saw her again. Soon after, Kyle disappeared. They heard he joined the Armed Forces, probably to piss his old man off. The Fowlers had plans for their children; they wanted doctors in the family.

Then Jared left town himself, joined the Navy, and lost touch with his old buddies. His mom had begged him not to go. He wasn't sure why he did, really. Except his old man had lived and breathed for the uniform. Maybe he thought he could figure out the big draw by trying it himself. And he had. The Navy opened up a whole new world for him. One filled with friendship and loyalty. A brotherhood. He'd never regretted his decision. Well, almost never.

"Thanks, man." Ty slapped him on the back, as he leaned over to gaze at his dream sound system. "I knew all that screwing around with computers was going to come in handy some day. I want it to be flawless, Jare. Look at these lights; they retract into the ceiling when not in use. That way I can preserve the old world look, but with a modern twist. And here," his excitement was contagious. "I'm going to hide the front of the speakers behind these specially made stained glass frames. They're cantilevered so the sound will pass right through without those ugly brown boxes on the wall."

Ty flipped to the second set of diagrams. "This though, this is the *pièce de résistance*. What do you think?" He looked up from the paper, enthusiasm lighting his eyes.

Jared wanted to tell him he was crazy for caring so much, but he couldn't. "Is that a sunken stage?"

"Yeah, that's exactly what it is. I went to a show in Seattle a few years ago, they had one there. I loved it, almost missed the whole show checking it out. I can do this, Jared. I know I can. See here, it's all on hydraulics. The whole platform lifts or lowers by the touch of a button. With this set-up the theatre will be perfect for either live performances or films. Maybe this time old man Fowler will keep it running." Ty pulled a thick carpenter's pencil from his pocket. "I just need to figure this one section out, right..."

Jared stood back as his friend lost himself in the restoration process. He turned and watched as the other workmen clambered up ladders and platforms around the room. This was no half-dash effort. Ty was putting everything he had into this project. Jared only hoped Katy would appreciate the meaning behind it when he finished.

Jared knew all about first love. He had his own Achilles' heel, Annie Campbell. Not that she'd ever known it. They'd been friends, pals, even lovers once. Fascinated by the shy, bookworm girl who sat in front of him in grade ten science period, he'd spent many a class staring at all the variations of cinnamon the sun brought out in her hair. Its silky golden, red-brown waves changed with every slight movement of her body, a glorious waterfall of color. Sweet and sexy, Annie Campbell.

Just then his cell rang from the depths of his pocket. *Who the hell...?* "Martin."

"Oh, Jared, I'm glad I caught you. Something's wrong with Annie. I know you're just down the road and hoped you could check on her." His momma's worry carried through the lines. "I tried getting hold of Jack—Sheriff Garrett—but he's out at the Henderson farm, you remember them don't you? Anyway, they have a cougar out there and called him out, so it'd be at least an hour before he can make it back in. I don't want her alone that long."

Jared tensed. Why would she need a cop? "Mom, tell me what's going on. I'm on the way."

He dropped the phone from his ear for a quick second. "Something has happened to Annie. I have to go."

"Yeah, of course," Ty said, worry creasing his brow. "Let me know later, hey."

"I will. Thanks, man."

Jared had already spun away. Long strides carried him out of the building as he brought the phone back to his ear to hear, "...stabbed."

What!

"Mom, I missed that. What did you say?" He ran, by-passing his truck in favor of a quick sprint up Main. What did she mean, stabbed? Jared's heart pounded so hard in his ears he could barely hear her.

"Hurry, son. Just hurry."

CHAPTER NINE

Sergei's lips curled with scorn, his breath a little cloud in front of him as he left the craft store and moved up the quiet morning street of the little town. He'd scared her. Good. Jared Martin needed to know he wasn't playing a game. The way he'd suffered disgrace at the hands of that man was unacceptable. He wanted his honor back. The only way it would happen was by making Martin pay.

Chenglei had come through with the information on Martin's whereabouts as promised—for a price. He wanted much more than what they'd originally agreed upon, but Sergei didn't care. His priority was to prove himself worthy to his Brigadier. He hadn't worked himself up to his position in the organization only to be defeated by some know-it-all American hustler.

The next task on his list was to pay a little visit to the eating-house down the street. Chenglei assured him this was an important place in Martin's past. Sergei planned on destroying everything Martin cared about, make him suffer, and finally put an end to his worthless life. It was the only way. He'd been a laughingstock ever since last spring when Jared Martin entered the casino and proceeded to rob them of close to eight hundred thousand dollars. He'd insisted he'd done nothing wrong, but Sergei knew different. They'd roughed the American up to teach him a lesson, then shoved him out the door. The next thing Sergei knew, sprinklers were drenching guests who were fighting to grab tickets spewing out of flashing slot machines, while fire alarms screamed their displeasure.

The humiliating incident made national news, angering his bosses. He'd paid with his blood. And now Jared Martin would pay with his.

Shock held Annie in frozen horror. All she could see was that knife flying past her head to land in poor Lulu-Belle. She couldn't take her gaze off it. The knife had embedded itself almost to the hilt. She was so cold she pulled her knees in tight to her chest and rocked in place. Tears streamed down her face to drip off her jaw, her nose ran, and all she could think was what if Chris had been with her?

Oh, God, Oh, God, Oh God.

She jumped up and ran to the phone. Her fingers shook so much it was hard to dial. Nothing like this was supposed to happen in her town. Tidal Falls had always been a safe place to raise children, a place where everyone knew each other. But not him. Annie had never seen that man before. His accent wasn't one she recognized, and his speech suggested he was still learning English. She swiped her face with the sleeve of her shirt, suddenly impatient with herself. She had more backbone than this. No one had gotten hurt—well, except for poor Lulu-Belle. It was time to quit feeling sorry for herself and get this place cleaned up. She still had a store to run. She'd better call Jack too, before he heard it from someone else. And a locksmith. She could see now where he'd jimmied her lock to get into the store.

"Cascade Elementary, how may I direct your call?"

Annie was relieved to hear the voice of one of her oldest friends, Rebecca Sorenson. "Hi Becky, it's me, Annie. Sorry to be a bother but can you check on Chris and Jessica Reed for me?"

"Of course I can, but they're a little young to be playing hooky." Rebecca teased. "Just give me a second, okay?" A switch clicked and elevator music drifted into Annie's ear. Normally she liked the soothing tones, today it ramped up her anxiety to near screaming proportions.

C'mon, c'mon, be there.

The music stopped and Becky's amused voice came back online, "They're fine, Mom. It's art time, seven kinds of chaos. Both Chris and Jessica are elbows deep in modeling clay. What's going on?"

That's what she wanted to know. "Just one of those days, you know how it goes. I'm lucky my head's attached or I'd be wondering where it was also." Annie thanked her and promised to meet next week for lunch before hanging up to call the police station. She found out Jack was at the restaurant grabbing a quick lunch. Hoping to catch him before he left on his afternoon runs, Annie dialed Grace's.

"Grits and Grace, if you're not here, you outta be. How can I help you?" Grace's homey voice almost brought on more crying. She cleared her tear-clogged throat, firmed her knees and gripped the phone a little harder.

"Grace, it's Annie. Is Jack still around by chance?" She kept her gaze off the mannequin.

"You catching a cold, sugar? No, honey, I'm sorry. Old man Henderson called just as he sat down to eat—doesn't that about figure. Guess they have a cougar problem out there they want him to handle. Don't ask me why it couldn't wait till the man got some lunch." She heaved a disgusted sigh. "He'll be there all afternoon, no doubt. Was it something important, honey-child? You could probably catch him on his cell before he gets too far."

Well, dang. She could probably get one of the deputies to come and take a statement, but she'd really wanted Jack. This was too personal. Silly, but she felt violated. Her safe place wasn't safe anymore.

"No, I don't want to bother him. It's not as if I'm the one who got stabbed."

"What! What did you say? You stay right there. Lock your door. I'm calling Jared right now." Slam went the phone before Annie could stop her. Great, now she'd have to deal with him *and* Spooky Guy.

She began the process of collecting the rest of the blades from where they'd scattered across the floor. Maybe knives weren't such a good idea. She could start out slower to build her male clientele. Wood-burning kits, or fly-tying maybe. Something a little less deadly.

A nervous giggle turned into a scream when the door flew back on its hinges, hitting the wall. The knives she'd gathered went flying for the second time even as her feet fought to gain traction on the linoleum and propel her out of range.

"Annie! Annie, it's me." Jared's worried cry slowed her forward momentum. Her heart settled back into her chest as she turned to see him silhouetted in the doorway. Her shoulders slumped and she breathed in a heartfelt sigh of relief.

"Swear to God, I think I lost ten years off my life this morning." She tried, without much success, to make light of her obvious fear. The old Annie would have gone running into the comforting arms of her best friend without a thought. This Annie held herself stiff. Alone.

"What the hell happened?" Jared demanded, his gaze sweeping the mess on the floor before he strode across to stand in her space. "Are you hurt? Ma said something about you being stabbed." His hand moved to gently lift her chin. His fingers tightened their grip when he saw her tears. "Annie, talk to me. What's going on?"

"I'm fine. I had a disgruntled customer this morning, no big deal." She pulled out of his grasp. "You didn't need to come, Jared, it could have waited." Not wanting to meet his gaze, she instead focused on his tattoos. Some she recognized, some were new. The tribal ink and anchor with a rope around it peeking from the edge of his sleeve she remembered well. But the frog skeleton was new, as was the heart she could just make out on the inside of his wrist as it dropped to his side. She'd always loved his tattoos, they were a part of him. He'd once told her he didn't care what people said, his tats told a story. One of dreams, beliefs, and memories. They triggered memories for her also.

"This seems like more than some ticked off client. Ma said you were hurt. Let me have a look." He went to touch her again, and she backed away. She was feeling a little too fragile. If he kept being so nice he was liable to have a bawling woman on his hands.

"Not me, Lulu-Belle," she said, waving a hand over her shoulder. Annie still wasn't quite stable enough to check out her mannequin with equanimity, so she looked to Jared for his reaction instead. His gaze looked perplexed to begin with—no doubt because there were only the two of them in the room—then as he followed the line of her fingers his eyebrows climbed to Mt. Everest proportions before diving towards the bridge of his nose. His blue eyes shot sparks from behind the lens of his glasses.

"What the fuck?" Jared shot her an angry look before he strode over to the dummy. "I thought you said an irate customer, this is way past irritated. What the hell happened here?" He frowned over his shoulder before pulling a rag out of his back pocket, wrapping it carefully around the hilt of the knife and yanking it out of poor Lulu-Belle.

Annie cringed at the sucking noise and the crude hole left behind. When Jared turned with the knife in hand she took an involuntary step back, though she knew he'd never hurt her. She suddenly realized she'd been wringing her hands and forced them down to her sides. If only she'd had time for coffee this morning. She'd known it was going to be one of those days. Too bad fate had to go and prove her right.

Jared set the knife on the nearby counter, and paced back to her side. "Okay, let's start at the beginning. Why do you have a case of knives in a craft store?"

"I thought we could take some combat training, never know when you might need it." She glared up at him, suddenly unreasonably angry. "I wanted to gain some male clientele, if you must know. Though at the moment, I'm not sure why."

He had the temerity to smile at her, like she was kidding.

"Look, I was in the process of carrying this shipment out front when some guy—who doesn't believe in closed signs, or locked doors for that matter—scared the bejesus out of me." She rubbed her hands up and down goose-bumpy arms. "I asked him what he wanted and he played all dark and mysterious. Had some kind of weird foreign accent. Creepy." She gave a nervous chuckle.

"Hey, don't play tough girl with me. You have a right to be upset." He grasped her cold fingers in his warm hands and gave a little squeeze. "The asshole was pretty brave, right on Main Street in broad daylight."

"Yeah well, he didn't seem too concerned. He dressed like some kind of fifties thug in a big trench coat and hat; probably pulled them off when he left here. I couldn't describe him if I wanted to." She shivered a little, remembering the cold intent in those dark eyes.

"I don't get it. Why would a guy like that break into a craft store? What did he want?"

Annie looked up and met Jared's worried gaze, "You. He wanted you."

CHAPTER TEN

DEA agent, Maggie Holt woke up groggy. The stench of unwashed bodies and moans of pain told her nothing had changed. For one brief moment she'd hoped everything that happened in the last few days was all a bad dream. But even before her gaze focused on the room, she knew. This was her new reality. It was difficult to fight back the hopelessness threatening to undermine her determination to be free.

When the prostitutes first began disappearing from the Vegas strip months ago, they'd come up with the plan for her to go undercover, see what she could find out. Was it related to the drug case they'd been working, or something more sinister? Everything on the street was quiet, hushed. Then she heard of a couple shelters for teens missing their regulars and realized the situation was worse than originally thought. Into the middle of this, they found ties to Adam's old SEAL team, creating a real clusterfuck. The DEA had already been following his team on what they thought was an unrelated matter, now she wasn't so sure. The more they investigated the more all roads seemed to lead in one direction, their own government.

She viewed the seemingly endless row of beds. The women hunched up like broken shells threatened to pull her under. Each cot came with one thin mattress, a gray army blanket, a flat pillow—and chains. The restraints gave her the most problems at the moment. The manacles binding her wrists above her head stopped her from getting to the clasp. She knew how to pick a lock, had practiced for hours as a child, but not like this. She'd rubbed her skin raw trying.

Her captors had boarded up the one high window in the room and left a row of flickering fluorescents on twenty-four seven, so she had no idea how much time had passed since she'd arrived. Only that she was not the last woman captured. Cot number ten down the way had been empty. It wasn't anymore. A young girl, she didn't look more than fifteen, stared with bleak, empty eyes, her face swollen from crying. Maggie wanted to reassure her, tell her it was going to be all right, but she couldn't bring herself to lie. It wasn't all right. In fact, she had a feeling if she didn't do something soon, they were all going to think this was a vacation compared to what came next.

Her stomach still felt queasy from whatever they shot into all the women's systems to keep them quiet. Judging by her dry mouth and bouts of dizziness she figured Diazepam, but wasn't sure.

The guard would be in to check on them soon. The women were unchained one at a time for a bathroom break. She needed to figure out a way to make the manacle looser when he reattached it to her wrist. She'd managed to work a spring out of the aging mattress beneath her and hide it in her pillowcase earlier when they'd been allowed to sit and eat a meal of thick, tasteless porridge.

The sound of a key scraping the lock had all eyes focusing in dread on the door. The girls never knew whether they'd be next, dragged out of the room, never to return. Maggie blocked it as much as she could, but a random tremor refused to be subdued. She couldn't go through that again. Neither could the rest of them, especially the new kid, who'd started to sob.

"Stop. You'll only make it harder on yourself. They love to pick on the weak ones." Maggie hissed the words, just as the door swung open. Great, it was Romeo.

The man seemed to think he was God's gift to women. Maggie had news for the guy. The slicked back, greaser hairstyle went out in the sixties. As had the bright silk shirts he favored, and the disgustingly tight jeans. The girl was still crying, softer now, but he'd notice. Gritting her teeth, Maggie sent her a warning glare before lifting her head and calling out, "Hey, it's about time. What's a girl gotta do around here to go to the can?"

It worked. She'd gotten his attention.

Damn.

He sauntered across the room as if he had all the time in the world. A smile revealed a gold-capped tooth he stroked with his tongue. Maggie choked back the bitter tasting bile in her throat. When he reached her side, he stood looking down at her for a long moment, and then he grabbed the dirty gray blanket and swept it aside.

Maggie went to her happy place. The place where she wasn't spread-eagled on a cot wearing her birthday suit while some creep ogled her and fondled himself.

"Well, well, what do we have here? If you want to use the *facilities,* Bonita, ahead of all these others..." His gaze swept the room, but thankfully missed the girl, who'd finally, *finally,* figured out she better keep quiet, "you'll have to earn it. Any idea how you're going to do that?" A smirk twisted his lip over that damn tooth, and lust gleamed from dark eyes. He lifted the hand that had just cupped his privates—*EW*—and trailed it along her ribcage to just under her breast.

Maggie sucked in a hard breath and tried not to cringe away from the SOB. The only way to protect the girl and distract the jerk was if he thought he might actually get lucky. The guards were warned to leave the girls alone. All except her. The boss, Chenglei, decided he wanted to keep her for his own pleasure. Him and his guests. A violent shiver rattled her body, and Romeo's eyes focused on her puckering nipples.

She coughed a little to clear her throat, and make him look her in the face. "You untie me and we can have some fun, I promise. *After* I go to the bathroom." Her voice came out husky from a lack of water. He hurried to dig through his pockets for the keys. His crotch was right at eye level as he reached over her head to undo the manacles. She turned away from his obvious erection. Her gaze went to the teen, who looked rightfully scared, then by a couple of the others who stared at Maggie in disgust. She lifted her chin in reply. If they wanted to believe she would willingly...

Whatever.

The chains rattled loose and the manacles dropped away, allowing her arms to drop to the pillow. She couldn't suppress her moan. She drew them down and covered her bare chest. Her captor laughed, and stepping back, waved a hand in the direction of the narrow little washroom. She swung her feet to the cool cement floor thankful her legs bore her weight, and stumbled down the row of beds, looking neither left nor right. She couldn't bear to see the women's disparaging gazes, this was hard enough.

There was no door on the tiny room. They'd all had to learn to overcome their embarrassment and attend to nature with the guards watching their every move. Humiliation at its finest. Lover‑boy attempted to follow her in. Maggie put on her game face, turned, and placed her hand upon his muscular chest.

"I want to get cleaned up a little, do you mind?" She licked her lips and made doe eyes at him.

He hesitated for a couple of minutes, and then shrugged. "Don't take all day, or I might have to pay a visit to your roommate." His gaze went straight to the girl.

Shit.

"Hey now, she wouldn't know how to please a big gorgeous guy like you," Maggie pouted, turning on the charm. "Not like I can." Her fingers grazed his jaw, turning his attention back to her. She reached up and kissed his dry lips, shriveling on the inside. He grasped her arms and pulled her up hard to his chest, deepening the connection. His hands had just settled on her bare bottom when she broke away with a frantic laugh.

She backed into the bathroom, twirling her hand in an effort to get him to give her a moment's privacy. He gave her a hungry stare, then abruptly swung around, too far from the entry for her to coldcock.

Her heart pounded in her breast like a captured bird. No time to waste. Maggie did her business, and then moved to the grimy sink with the pitted mirror. She couldn't look into her eyes. Instead she took inventory of her face. Her skin looked too pale and her hair was a matted mess, but otherwise normal. How was that possible? She should look how she felt. Old. Dead inside. She hated the things that bastard Chenglei, had forced her to do. Shivering, she turned on the rusty hot water and slid her hands under, gasping as the heat burned against raw wrists. But the pain felt good—it meant she was alive.

"Hurry up, time's a ticking." His voice jarred, made her want to scream her frustration. Where was Adam? Why hadn't he found her yet?

"Enough, you're wasting time. Come here, sugar." Rough, calloused hands bruised her forearms, pulling her away from the now cooling water. His teeth nipped at the tender skin on the side of her neck, and her back bowed as he pushed her belly into the sink from behind. Maggie battled the instinct to flee. She had to get him to do something with the cameras; it was the only way.

She leaned forward, just enough for his hard-on to nestle her ass for a too-long moment, then straightened putting as much distance between them as she could. "I'm ready, but don't you think you'd better douse the video? The boss warned you the last time." She held her breath and watched him in the mirror, hoping he'd take the bait.

Strategically placed cameras covered every square inch of space, including the open washroom. She counted on his little head to be doing the thinking, otherwise he'd realize he was courting death by defying Chenglei. He'd been lucky before, and only received a tongue-lashing from another guard for sneaking a kiss. She, on the other hand, had not escaped punishment.

Maggie forced the fear aside, she needed to do something. Time was running short for them. She could sense his indecision and decided to help matters along. Her hands went up as if to pull the hair away from her face. His fingers tightened where they'd landed on her hips, his gaze following the lift of her breasts in the mirror. It was enough. Whirling, he grabbed the brown hand towel and in a couple of strides, threw it over the nearest camera.

"Now, where were we?" He undid his pants as he moved towards her, his smile resembling a shark circling before a feast. His brawny arms wrapped her body, tugging her forward.

Maggie slid her arms around his neck and leaned in close to his ear. "Here. We were here." And she thrust the straightened spring into his carotid artery.

CHAPTER ELEVEN

They stood close together in the dimness of the craft store. Jared stared down into Annie's misty green eyes and fought the urge to pull her into his arms. The citrus shampoo she'd used filled his mind with memories of his hands combing through her silky curls. The taste of her sweet lips. The feel of her luscious body wrapped around him in pleasure.

And he'd let her go.

His gut twisted into knots. Why would anyone want to break into a little craft store? It wasn't likely to have much cash on hand, and unless the guy was into knitting there wasn't much in the way of valuables either. Suddenly the rest of what she'd said fell into place.

"Where's your son?" His hold on her hands tightened. She looked pale, frightened. It was his fault. If that prick had harmed one hair on her head... "Tell me again. What exactly did he say?"

"He said to tell you there's no place you can hide. And he wants repaid, whatever that means." Annie frowned and pulled one hand free to rub the back of her neck. She straightened her spine. "Chris is fine, he's at school. Anyway, Jack will be here soon and I'll give a statement. Let him handle this, Jared, he knows what he's doing."

And I don't? Is that what she thought? What did she think he'd been doing for the past eight years? Jared spun away before he said something he'd regret and paced over to the glass door. He took inventory of the busy street. Everything looked normal. He drew in a deep breath, needing a moment to get his frustration under control. She was only giving voice to what the whole town thought, but from her more than any other, it hurt.

Annie moved to his side. "Look, I'm sorry. That was uncalled for. I just want to handle this by the book. It was nothing more than a simple break and enter. Jack will catch the guy and then we can forget this ever happened, okay?" she pleaded, lifting her hand to touch his arm.

He tensed in response. But then she let it drop and something within him fell with it. He wished...he wished they could go back eight years to that next morning so he could have another chance. He really did.

Jared figured his old friend Sergei had managed to track him to Tidal Falls. The overcoat thing Annie mentioned confirmed it, if not the accent. He'd seemed to enjoy wandering around the casino looking like a mafia hit-man. Damn Russian. Jared regretted ever getting mixed up with the Golden Key.

After receiving his discharge papers he'd decided to move to Las Vegas with the half-baked plan to start up a security company after taking a little time to wind down. He'd heard about some high stakes games going on at the Key and decided to try his luck. The place rocked, full of socialites and wealthy businessmen. Jared won a few grand and returned often over the next couple months, making friends with the dealers. Then came the fateful night. He'd always been good with numbers. When he noticed some discrepancies in the cards, he started counting. One thing led to another and next thing he knew he was hustled to a back room and physically warned against returning by head of security, Sergei the Serious. Jared's Scottish temper got the best of him, and he retaliated by screwing with their mainframe computer system. The cops hadn't liked his reasoning, or the pandemonium that broke out when he set off the casino's fire alarms and caused winning tickets to spew forth out of almost every VLT in the place. He'd ended up on probation and been warned against any more gambling. Just as well, it was time to get serious about setting up his business anyway. He'd been looking at locations when Nick called.

"You're not mad, are you?" Annie's voice at his elbow snapped his attention back to the here and now. If Sergei was here, how had he known to come after Annie? And if he knew about her, what about...Ma.

"I need to check on my mother. Come on, let's go." He pushed open the door and waved her through, frowning when she didn't budge. "What? I'm not leaving you here, so just forget it."

Her head shook, curls flying, even as she gazed with worried eyes up the street to Grits and Grace. "I can't, Jared. The creep ruined my lock. Everything I have is in this store. I can't leave it unattended." She turned grass green eyes up to him. "I'll be fine, Jack will be here right away. Go, please. Make sure Grace is safe."

He hesitated, torn between the need to check on his mom, and the overwhelming desire to keep Annie safe. A moment later the decision was made for him as a siren's scream rent the air and a cop car roared around the corner and squealed to a stop on the wrong side of the street in front of The Craft Shack. The sheriff swung open his door almost before the car came to a halt. He grabbed his hat off the dash and jammed it on his head as he climbed out and started for the store. When Jack caught sight of the two of them by the door he paused, a frown pulling his eyebrows into rigid lines over his brow.

"Annie, you okay?" Jack's brown-eyed gaze stayed focused squarely on Jared except for a quick up and down catalog of Annie's body, his hand firm on his weapon.

"I'm fine, Jack. The guy's gone." Annie brushed by Jared, moving between the two men. "We're attracting attention. Do you think you can turn off the lights now?"

The sheriff held his rigid stance for a moment longer, then reached in and snapped off the flashing red and blues. He grabbed his radio, canceled the callout, slammed his door and moved up to Annie's side. "What happened, honey?"

Jared stiffened.

"I'm not really sure. I was getting ready to open, unpacking some new stock...I got those knives in I told you about," Annie stammered the words out, shivering as reaction obviously started to set in. Jared started toward her, but Jack was already pulling her into his arms. Jared clenched his jaw and folded empty arms across his chest, rocking back on his heels.

"Take your time." Jack rubbed his palm up and down her spine, his gaze narrowed on Jared. "Why don't we all go inside and I'll have a look around while you explain what happened."

Not on your life.

Jared had no intention of being a third wheel. Besides, he was still worried about his mom. "Looks like you have everything under control, *Sheriff.*" He congratulated himself for keeping most of the sarcasm out of his voice. "I'll leave you to it. My stomach's saying it's long past lunchtime." Annie turned and opened her mouth. He gave a slight shake of his head, asking for her silence.

She frowned, and he figured he'd be spending the day at the cop shop, but then she spun on her heel and strode back toward the building. "C'mon, Jack. Wait until you see what a good carving knife can do."

Jack looked as if he wanted to arrest Jared, just on principle. "Stick around, Martin. I might have questions for you later."

"Yeah, I know the routine, I'm not going anywhere. Just make sure you do your job. Find this guy and we won't need to have that talk." Jared hesitated another second, loathe to leave Annie behind. The sheriff moved to follow her into the store and he shrugged. Point taken, they didn't need him here. He strode up the street toward Grits and Grace, and kept an eye peeled for the grim reaper, aka Sergei the Annoying. No sign of the caped crusader. Just as well, in the mood he was in after finding the knife embedded in that freaking doll, Jared didn't want to lay odds on a civilized conversation taking place. The man was seriously getting on his last nerve. It was one thing to threaten him over a perceived wrongdoing, but this was over the top. The guy was a psycho.

When Jared arrived at the café, he was relieved to see the place half full. A little hard for the Russian to pull anything that way. Still, he wanted to see his momma, just to be sure. He pulled open the door, and had to smile at the song playing on the jukebox, "Teddy Bear." He'd always loved old Red Sovine. Susan gave him a little wave with the coffeepot as he moved down the aisle. People he vaguely recognized called out his name like they were glad to see him, and the smell of fresh baked cinnamon buns led him straight back to the kitchen. There she sat, on her favorite stool, rolling little rounds of dough with those agile fingers of hers, making dinner rolls. Jared had spent hours watching her magically make buns, laugh with customers through the window, and cook meals all at once. She fascinated him, this woman who'd given birth to a child who never appreciated all her sacrifices. He did now.

"Hi, Momma." He watched her head come up, a look of such love moving over her face and lighting her eyes, his own teared up. *Why had he stayed away so long?*

"Jared, how are you, son? Is Annie okay? We could see the lights from the sheriff's car down the block. What happened?" She slipped off the stool and had to grab the counter for a moment to regain her balance. He hurried to her side and grasped her arm.

"Mom, what's wrong?" His voice came out gruff as he frowned down at her.

She laughed it off. "Nothing, I'm fine. Just get a little dizzy now and then. I'm not getting any younger, you know." She teased and chucked him under the chin with buttery fingers.

"Mom." He swiped the grease and held her steady. "Have you been to see the doc?"

"That old quack? I'm better off diagnosing myself," Grace growled. "I just need a glass of juice, that's all. Let me wash up and we'll go sit for a minute so you can tell me everything."

He eased back but kept a close watch as she moved to the deep double sink and turned on the faucet. She looked pale. He'd better have a talk with Susan, find out what was going on. Grace dried up, grabbed a couple of plates and loaded them up with gooey, still warm, sticky buns.

"This'll fix what ails me, c'mon, son." She nodded toward the front and he had no choice but to let the matter drop. For now.

Rattled, Annie wasn't sure why she kept silent and let Jared walk away. She didn't owe him a darn thing. Holding secrets wasn't her style. Well, except for Chris.

She hurried into the store, only to come to a stumbling halt just inside the entrance. Sunlight shone through the big display windows and landed squarely on the mortally wounded dummy. The poor thing didn't even have any clothes on to cover the garish hole in its chest.

Where was she going to find another Lulu-Belle? Annie had come to think of the mannequin as her good luck charm. She'd found her in an old warehouse sale in Seattle years ago, not long after buying the craft store. Lulu-Belle had been front and center through all of her ups and downs of learning a business. She was family.

The smell of pine announced Jack's closeness just before warm hands landed on her shoulders. Annie jumped a little. She sucked in a long, slow breath, and then let it out before turning his way. "Thanks for coming so fast, Jack. How did you hear?"

"Grace called the Henderson's. I headed right back. You should have called the office. One of the others could have arrived here quicker," he chided, his fingers massaging the tension from her muscles.

"I wanted you." As soon as she said it, she knew it was the wrong thing to say. His eyes flared in response, obviously taking the words in the wrong context. He went to pull her into his arms. She quickstepped sideways with a nervous laugh and motioned to the mannequin, ignoring his perplexed gaze. "Look what that creep did to poor Lulu-Belle. With my carving knife yet."

At the mention of the knife Jack's gaze flew to the gaping hole in the dummy. "Holy shit." He strode over to the doll, pulled his cell out, and then proceeded to snap pictures like a crazed paparazzi.

"You can say that again," she said, half under her breath.

"Hmm?" His attention remained riveted on the wound. "Where's the weapon? Did he take it with him?" Jack's fingers were already on the dial pad, when she pointed to the counter.

"No, it's there, in that cloth. Jared pulled it out."

"He what?" Anger flashed across Jack's face. "What the hell did he do that for? He should be arrested for tampering with evidence. Didn't they teach him anything in that fancy Navy school?" Jack shook his head and moved to the counter, pulling a set of white latex gloves from his belt. He carefully pulled back the edges of the cloth and whistled. "This is one of the carving knifes you ordered?" He glanced her way.

"Yeah, why?"

"You could slice a turkey with these, sugar. I'm not so sure you'd want to advertise them as wood carving tools. You might end up with a lawsuit on your hands."

Well, isn't that just the end to a perfect day?

CHAPTER TWELVE

Romeo grasped his neck with both hands and fell against the wall, gurgling as he gasped for breath. The coppery smell of his blood, dark red as it poured between his fingers should have shaken Maggie. It didn't. Shock had set in, allowing her to step back from her actions. At least she hoped her time in this place hadn't totally destroyed her humanity. She gazed dispassionately as he slumped to the floor, his eyes gazing into her own in anger, then fright, before slowly turning dull and vacant.

She knelt beside the body to gingerly search for the keys to unlock the others. She kept her gaze focused on the job at hand and refused to acknowledge his last wet breaths. Then—nothing. Frustrated because everything was blurry and she couldn't see, Maggie swiped impatient fingers across her eyes, surprised to find they came away pink and damp. Panicking now, she jumped up, turned the taps on full force, and shoved her face right under the stream, desperate to erase his blood from her flesh. After long moments, she lifted her head, wiped again and then forced her hand into his pocket until she felt the keys. She wrestled them out of the snug cloth, then stood and moved around the widening pool of blood. Hurrying to the first bed, she unlocked the restraints from the woman's limp wrists and moved to the next, and the next. She was working on the young girl's locks when she glanced around and noticed no one had moved. They were all lying in the exact same positions as before.

"What are you doing?" she cried. "Get up. Hurry. We have to move. There isn't much time."

The young girl rose on shaky legs. Maggie wrapped the scratchy blanket around her shoulders before whirling toward the closed window. There was a small chance, if they could just get through that boarded-up glass. One chair sat in the corner, near the door. The guards used it while watching them eat. Maggie raced past the prone women, grabbed the chair and centered it below the window. Now she needed to find something to wedge under the boards. Her gaze feverishly swept the room. *The cameras.* They needed to cover the rest of the cameras. She yanked the grey sheet off the bed and threw it over the one camera. *One to go.* Desperate and angry, she jumped onto the bed below the last camera and ripped it from the wall, ignoring the gasp of the woman lying between her feet.

"Someone watch that door." Maggie snarled over her shoulder.

Finally, two of the women rose and made their way to the door on wobbly legs, and just like that, Maggie's rage disappeared. They were victims, all of them. She got down from the bed, careful not to jostle the girl lying there and searched the room again for something to pry the wood.

Nothing. There's nothing here, damn it.

Frustration curled viciously through her chest, tightening her lungs until she could barely draw breath. She jumped onto the chair and dug her fingers under the edge of the wood, frantic to get enough of a grip to pull it free. Slivers pierced her flesh, but she barely noticed, all her focus on the small patch of light she could just see between the boards.

"Here, try this."

Maggie turned. It was Olga, the oldest of the women. She'd been in this shithole the longest and was Maggie's predecessor for Chenglei's dubious attentions. Chenglei liked to foster dissent among the women by picking favorites and showering them with gifts of better food, clothing, and soap. As if any payment could recompense the women for the loss of self-esteem. However, it had worked to undermine Maggie's efforts to investigate. She'd tried repeatedly to gain the women's trust, to no avail. So now she knew the endgame, but was no closer to closing down this ring.

"Do you want it, or not?"

Maggie looked down into Olga's bland stare and wondered what drove a once beautiful young woman into a life of prostitution. A Swedish heritage had stamped lines of pride on the woman's high cheekbones and sky blue eyes. Her thick blond hair hung lank down her bare back. Her ribs were prominent against her concave stomach, but her posture remained unbowed.

"Here, take this before I decide you're as crazy as I think you are and use it on you."

Maggie caught the glint of steel and whipped her hand around the other woman's wrist. The wrist attached to the hand holding a knife. Upon closer examination she saw it was only a butter knife, but still.

"Where did you get this?" She shook Olga's arm slightly. "How did you get it in here? They haven't given us anything except plastic spoons to eat with."

"Does it matter? I have it; you need it. Are we going to have an interrogation, or get the hell out of here?" Olga opened her palm and the knife lay there like an offering, almost too good to be true.

Maggie hesitated. The little reference to questioning had her wondering, did she know? Did the rest of them? Maggie searched their eyes but only found frightened hope. Her heart pounded; if this didn't work she was afraid it would be too late. They'd all be sold off to the highest bidder and never seen again. Adam would turn the earth over to locate her, she knew that, but it would be fruitless if Chenglei shipped them out to some European country. That's what this was after all, a human trafficking ring stretching all across North America and Europe. Whenever Chenglei placed her on display for his friends she'd listened and learned. They obviously felt themselves invincible because they never even tried to conceal their conversations from her. All except the Russian.

Maggie shivered, and taking the knife, nodded a short thanks before getting back to the boards with renewed enthusiasm. *Better.* Now that she could actually chip away at the wood, the strip of light grew brighter. One plank fell, then another. She could see outside for the first time in weeks. Tears blurred her vision and she impatiently rubbed her face against her shoulder. It was late afternoon, the sun was almost at eye level, indicating maybe four or five o'clock. They were facing west onto a field of high grass with a stand of evergreens in the distance, maybe a mile away. *So, a farm then.* How far would they have to go for help? It didn't matter; ten miles or a hundred, if it meant freedom.

"Quick, I need a blanket." She called over her shoulder. A hand tentatively touched her side. Maggie glanced down to see the teen strip the coarse wool from her body and hand it up with shaking fingers and trusting eyes. Maggie wanted to yell at her don't—don't trust anyone. Instead she took the blanket with a gentle smile and wrapped it around her arm.

"Okay, here goes nothing. Get back." With that she put every inch of power left in her body into her elbow and slammed it against the window. There was a little explosion and then glass rained down around her and sweet, fresh air blew into the room. Maggie closed her eyes and breathed out a silent prayer of thanks.

"Hand me one of those boards, I need to clear these shards away so we can get through."

"Quick, I hear voices." The taller of the two by the door cried.

Damn it, they only needed a few more minutes. Careful of where she stepped, Maggie got down, cradling her numbed arm. She reluctantly left the promise of escape to carry the chair back to the door amid moans of despair, and jammed it under the knob. Olga, catching on, took the discarded blanket and laid it doubled under the window to protect their bare feet.

The doorknob rattled amid angry shouts.

"Go," Maggie shouted, pressing against the door. "They'll be through soon. Hurry."

Olga shared one last look of sad understanding with her before wheeling to place her hands on the wall. "Climb my back." And when the women hesitated, "C'mon, do you want this to be the end? *Move.*" The teen stumbled forward and the others helped her scramble up the human stepladder until she could slither through the open window. She flipped over and held her hands for the next one through, desperate hope lighting her young face.

The door bucked against Maggie's back and she knew there were only seconds left. *Not enough time. There's not enough time.*

She took one last glance at escape and turned away, plastering her hands against the door in a futile effort to hold the battering at bay.

"Run, Maggie, run." Olga yelled over the sound of splintering wood.

CHAPTER THIRTEEN

Annie's customers began to appear at the door of the shop, curiosity lighting their features when the deputy Jack had called in informed them of the crime scene.

Crime scene.

How could her cute little store be a crime scene?

The world as she knew it had turned upside down. Annie craved security. She liked to know when she got up in the morning she'd take Chris to school, stop, grab a coffee and a chat at Grace's, then spend the rest of the day doing what she liked best, sharing her love of crafts.

Now she felt scared, cast adrift on a sea of insecurities. A little bit like the day she took Chris out fishing and they ended up stuck on an old country road after a flash rainstorm. She'd climbed out of her car to examine the situation and immediately sunk ankle deep in viscous clay. It took every ounce of strength she possessed to pull herself free and climb back into the car with a sunny expression on her face so as not to frighten her son. She was determined to do the same today, even if it killed her.

A short, older man dressed in faded coveralls and a railway cap arrived at the shop soon after Jared left. He introduced himself as the locksmith with instructions to install a security system. Annie looked to Jack, who shrugged. Jared must have made the call. She should be annoyed at him for taking control but instead could only feel gratitude. He'd appeared just when she'd needed him most. And the care he'd shown, making sure she was unharmed, that Chris was safe, standing so close...

"So you didn't get a good look at the perpetrator's face? Think, Annie. You haven't given me much to go on here." Jack's impatient words broke through her musings.

"Well, I don't know what else to say, Sheriff."

He looked up from his notes, a frown creasing his brow. She sighed. It wasn't Jack's fault some creep had scared the bejesus out of her.

"I'm sorry, Jack. I know you're just doing your job. I appreciate it, truly." She reached out and touched his hand before shoving cold fingers deep into her hoody. "I don't know what else to tell you. He looked like a mafia hit man from a low budget movie set. Ugly coat, uglier hat, and a God-awful command of the English language. That's about it."

He tapped his pen an annoying couple of times on the counter before closing the notebook and sliding it into his shirt pocket. "Okay, I'll get this written up and put an APB out on the guy, but I wouldn't hold your breath. He could be anywhere by now."

That was what scared her the most. Where did he go? What did he want? It was probably useless to hope he'd had a change of heart. Maybe realized the error of his ways and gone back to whatever cave he'd crawled out from.

"I understand. Thanks for coming so fast. Grace said you'd gone out to the Henderson's."

Jack sent her a chiding glance, his espresso-colored eyes solemn. "Of course I'd be here. I care about you, Annie. No matter what happens between us, never doubt that, okay?"

Tears welled up, clogging her throat. "Okay," she whispered.

Jared followed his mom to a quiet corner table and made sure she was safely seated before dropping down himself. At least her color was returning to normal, though she still looked wilted. He frowned, not liking the yellow tinge to her eyes. He waited for her to take a couple shaky sips of the juice Susan had brought, before broaching the subject. "You going to tell me what's going on with you?"

"I told you, nothing is going on. I just get a little tired sometimes. It's no big deal." She gazed everywhere but at him, until he stretched to clasp her clammy hand. Then she changed the subject. "Never mind about me, what happened with Annie? I've been worrying myself sick. I tried to call her but kept getting a busy signal. Is she hurt?"

"No, she's fine, a little shook up maybe." Jared didn't want to worry her but she needed to be aware of the possible danger. "Someone broke into her store, Mom."

"Oh no, my poor girl," Grace cried, pushing up from her chair. "I need to go check on her."

Jared gripped her wrist before she could charge out the door. "It's okay, she's not hurt. The sheriff is there right now. He'll take care of her." He swallowed down the sour taste of the words. "You can call her later. I'm sure she'll be happy to hear from you."

Grace hesitated but just then new customers came in. She sighed, "You're right, of course. Jack is a very capable young man. Well, as long as she's safe, it's back to work for me. I'll talk to you later, son." She leaned over and gave him a peck on the cheek before plodding away.

Jared's stomach twisted. He motioned Susan over, he wanted her to verify how bad it actually was. "Hey, pretty lady, do you have a minute?" He chuckled when she cuffed him on the shoulder and plopped down beside him.

"For you, honey, anytime. What's up?" Her gravelly voice reminded Jared Susan was getting up there in age also. She must be on the far side of fifty by now, too old to be running her butt off for this place, that's for damn sure.

"I'm worried about Ma. She doesn't look very good. She almost lost her balance in the kitchen a few minutes ago. What's going on, Sue?"

She fiddled with the washrag in her hands for a few moments, folding, and then refolding until he placed his own palm over the top, stopping her. "Look, I know she probably swore you to secrecy, but I have a right to know." He hesitated, almost afraid to put his fear into words. "It's cancer, isn't it?"

Susan gasped, "God no, whatever gave you that idea?" She turned her work-roughened hand over and clasped his tightly. "No, child. Your momma is fine. She has diabetes, that's all. If she doesn't pay enough attention to the time and forgets to have a snack, she gets dizzy." Susan smiled reassuringly, "It's a process, and we're still learning, but she's doing okay. Don't you worry; I won't let anything happen to your mom. Who else is going to cause me grief, huh?"

Jared sat back and let the relief wash over him. Diabetes was a serious disease and needed proper management or it could have dire consequences, but at least it was manageable. "You don't know how glad I am you said that. I was picturing…"

"Tut, tut, none of that now. We ain't ready to be pushing up daisies yet, my boy." Her gaze swept the restaurant, and then returned to him. "I won't lie to you. Grace ignored the problem for too long—you know how she is about doctors—and it cost her. Instead of an exercise and diet plan, she now has to take meds three times a day. But at least for now, that's it, no needles."

Jared's gut turned at the thought of poking himself. He must have looked a little green because she hastened to add, "Her blood glucose readings have been pretty good, in the sevens and eights. Not ideal, which is in the six point range, but not bad either. When she first went in they were sixteen. Doc Johnson wasn't impressed, let me tell you. They had a bit of a go-around, but then reached an agreement. She goes in for a checkup twice a year; he'll do his best to keep her feet planted on the ground."

"You telling stories again, old woman?" Susan and Jared jumped guiltily and turned to see Grace, fists clenched on her apron-clad hips and eyes snapping fire. "What have I told you about gossiping out of school? And you, Jared, you should be ashamed. If you want to know something, then ask. Don't go snooping behind my back. I thought we were past this kind of thing."

Jared felt his shoulders hunching and had to force himself to straighten. She still had it, even after all these years. Her lectures had always been more than enough punishment to leave him sorry for whatever perceived misdeed he'd done. Thirty-five years old and she could still make him quake in his seat. He shook his head, a wry smile twisting his lips, "C'mon, Mom. I had to ask Sue, you weren't going to tell me anything."

"Well, you're certainly right about that. It took you eight long years to come home, do you really think I want you worrying about me the second you get back?" Grace unfolded her fists, smoothed out her apron, pulled out another chair and sat beside him. "I'm sorry, son, old habits. As Susan probably already informed you," She sliced a glare across the table; Sue shrugged and looked sheepish. "I've developed type two Diabetes. But it's nothing a little diet and exercise can't keep under control, so don't either one of you worry none about me."

"Mom, it's in the job description. Of course we're going to be concerned. What would we do without you? You are, and always have been, our anchor. Even though I haven't done a very good job of showing you."

Instant tears welled to the surface of both women's eyes. Susan grabbed a couple napkins and passed one over. "He's right, you old coot. I need you too, so don't you up and die on me."

"Who said anything about death?" Grace huffed with an indignant lift of the chin. "I'm not going anywhere for a long time yet. Now are you going to serve our customers, or do I have to fire your butt?" Her lips wobbled into a somewhat damp smile.

Susan sniffled, wiped her eyes and hopped up like a woman half her age. "Promises, promises. I'm going now, you two sit here and make nice, you hear me?" She reached over and gave Jared a sloppy kiss on the cheek, then took off laughing and joking with the customers over the clash of the register.

Jared returned to scanning his mom's face. "So how have things been, Mom? Business good?"

"Oh, you know son, it has its ups and its downs. We're okay. A lot of businesses didn't do so well during the recession. Lucky for us, when people want a place to go and gripe, it's usually a restaurant they'll head for." She cast an eye over the room, waving at an elderly couple on their way out, the man's hand under his wife's elbow. "I love this place, Jared. It's my life. It scares me to think of giving it up."

"That's not going to happen. We'll work it out together, as a family. I'm here now, let me help. Please, Mom." His chest tightened at the defeated look on her face. He'd never once seen her ready to throw in the towel like this. It worried him.

She patted his cheek, "You're a good boy. I never told you that often enough, but you are. I pray you can make peace while you're here, Jared. I don't like to get into the middle of your affairs, I never have, but you need to have a talk with Annie."

He sat back, startled at the change of topic. What did she know about them? He'd never said a word about that night, or his growing feelings for his best friend either. He shouldn't be surprised. His mother always knew what he was thinking, almost before he did.

"I know. I will. There just hasn't been the right moment, yet. I'll catch up to her when this break and enter stuff winds down."

"Well don't wait too long. It's already been eight years." She stared at him meaningfully. "It's past time you three get this settled."

He froze. Was she saying what he thought she was saying? He was about to pump her for more information when the door opened ushering in a cool breeze and a tall, wide-shouldered man in a dark trench coat.

Sergei.

CHAPTER FOURTEEN

Jared listened with half an ear as his mom lectured him over staying away from home for too long. His gaze narrowed on the Russian interrogating the young server girl at the till. He had to give the man credit. Sergei was like a dog after a bone. And now he'd brought his petty differences to Tidal Falls. Jared had paid his restitution; so far as he was concerned it was finished.

"Mom, I gotta go. We'll talk about this later, all right?" He interrupted his mother's spiel, rose to his feet and made sure his body blocked her view of the doorway. "I'll call you tonight, I promise." His lips tightened at her look of resignation. When were they ever going to get things right between them? It was obvious in her sad gaze she expected him to disappear again. He deserved her disappointment, but it still hurt, dammit. "Make sure you wait for Susan and walk home together. You never know what kind of trash might be wandering around."

Jared strode toward Sergei, planning to get him out the door before he could get a look at the person he'd been sitting with. He cringed when her voice rang out. She had to get in the last word.

"This conversation isn't over, young man. You make sure you do what I told you, Jared. I love you."

His lifted his hand in acknowledgement. Sergei's gaze locked on him with recognition and filled with banked anger.

"Not here. Let's take this outside." Jared refused to allow a scene in the middle of Grace's, and held his breath as he brushed past the Russian, hoping he'd follow. Jared heaved a silent sigh of relief when he did and led the way around to the alley, glancing up at the now looming clouds on the horizon. He checked to make sure the back door was closed this time and they were alone, then turned to face his opponent, only to find a gun pointed at his midriff.

"Yeah, that's a great idea. Why don't you just shoot me and put me out of my misery? Then you can spend the rest of your days locked up in a six by six jail cell."

"Never let them see you sweat." Frank's voice rang in his ears. Easy for him to say, he wasn't staring down the barrel of a Makarov.

The new security system was in place and the store cleaned up and back to normal. Or as normal as it could be without Lulu-Belle, who'd been *taken in for questioning*—evidence. Annie grinned, hurrying down the walk toward the school. Jack hadn't seen the humor when she'd asked if her mannequin needed a lawyer. Jared would have gotten the joke. He had the same slightly warped sense of wit she did, and would've known she was just releasing stress with her off-the-wall comments. Jack had promised to have a patrol car cruise by a couple of times per shift until they caught the culprit. Annie hoped it wouldn't take long, she didn't like being nervous in her own town.

She breathed in crisp chilly air, bundled her coat a bit tighter, and tried to keep out of the cooler shadows next to the buildings. Before they knew it, winter would be upon them. She'd better look into buying Chris a new jacket and boots soon. Every time she turned around that boy grew another inch. He was going to be tall; like his father.

Now that she'd had some space to process Jared's return, Annie knew she had to talk with both of the men in her life. Jared deserved to know he was a father and Chris could only benefit from having another male figure to look up to in his young world. Jack was great with him, taking him to ball games and rides in the squad car, but nothing could compare to having your own father there for you; she should know. Annie only hoped Jared would get to know his son before he left again. Grace had mentioned he planned on staying this time, and she knew he'd gone to work for Ty, but in her heart she was doubtful. The men in her life never stayed.

The school came into sight and Annie sighed in relief; she wasn't late. A one story sprawling, cream color, it blended into the surrounding landscape like an old friend. She checked her watch, saw she still had half an hour before the bell rang, and climbed the front stairs to the door. May as well see if Rebecca had time for a chat.

The hush as she tiptoed through the hall to the office gave no warning of the chaos that would erupt when the end of the day bell sounded. Annie planned on being out by the bike stands by then; her usual spot for meeting her son.

Rebecca glanced up from her computer when the door opened and a smile lit her pretty face. The two of them had been friends since their time in Cascade Elementary and tried to get together at least once a month for a girls night out. Like herself, Rebecca was single, so they often consoled each other on the shortage of available men worth knowing in Tidal Falls. That was the problem with growing up in a small town, lack of choice.

"Hi, I was just thinking about calling you. Isn't your birthday next week? We should go out. Maybe to Seattle." Rebecca rested her chin on her palm, her raven hair picking up glints of blue from the overhead lighting. "Yeah, we could make a day of it. Shopping, dinner, and then a night on the town. What do you think? Say yes, it'll be fun."

Annie laughed. Rebecca provided a breath of fresh air. "Yes, yes, and yes. It is my birthday, as you very well know," she grinned. "Seattle sounds great, and a night on the town, divine. I'm in. Sara should be back by then, we'll see if she can join us. And how about Katy Fowler? She's getting married soon. I bet she could use a night out."

"Great idea, I haven't seen Katy since she came back to town. I heard she's been driving Ty crazy with getting the Twilight Theatre ready for the ceremonies." A sparkle lit her bright blue eyes. She pushed back her desk chair, rose and moved up to the other side of the counter. "Speaking of which," Rebecca's voice dropped to a near whisper, "I heard a rumor that Jared Martin is home. Spill, girlfriend. Have you seen him yet? How does he look? Hot as ever, I bet."

A mental picture of Jared as she'd seen him last filled Annie's mind. Standing so close they shared the same air, his scent of pine and warm male heating her insides. His gaze frank, worried. And filled with lust. God knows, she'd felt it too. The pull of chemistry between them seemed stronger than ever. Dangerous.

Hot? Oh yeah, he's hot.

Annie swallowed.

Rebecca smirked. "Never mind, I have my answer."

Annie's cheeks reddened. "How did we land on this topic anyway? I have more important news than Jared Martin. Do you want to hear it, or not?"

Rebecca outright laughed at that, then covered her mouth with her hand, glancing around to make sure they were still alone. "Sorry. Of course I want to hear your big news. What's up?"

Annie paused for dramatic impact, more than happy to change the subject. "I was broken into this morning."

"What? Are you freaking serious?" Becky's eyes grew saucer wide. "When? Were you there? Oh my God, Annie, that's terrible."

Warmed by her friend's support, Annie felt better for the first time all day. "I was there, and yes, it scared the hell out of me, but I'm fine now."

She did a quick twirl. "See? All in one piece. Jared came right over when I called Grace's looking for Jack. But by then the guy was long gone. Then Jack showed up and took a statement. They're looking for the creep now, so I'm sure it won't be long before he's caught."

Rebecca slumped in relief. "Why would anyone want to break into a craft store? Not to say you don't have nice stuff in there, but seriously? That's nuts."

Annie's lips quirked at the backhanded compliment. "I know, right." She held back from sharing what the man had said, the urge to protect Jared running strong. Until she knew more about what was going on, she'd keep quiet. "Maybe he's a closet knitter and isn't ready to come out with it to his family."

They both chuckled at the idiocy of the notion. Then Rebecca leaned over the counter, "So seriously, what was that like? Two big strong men come running to your rescue. It's a Victorian melodrama."

The blare of the bell saved Annie from replying. "Uh, oh. That's my cue. I'll talk to you next week. Maybe I'll have more to share by then." She waved and backed to the doorway.

"You better save up some juicy stories for your party. We'll want details, lots of details," Rebecca grinned, already moving to the school intercom system. "Okay kids, final bell. Don't forget your hats, coats, boots, and homework. See you tomorrow."

Annie hurried through the hallway, waving at other parents she knew. There were only a couple of children at the bike rack when she arrived. She blew out a relieved breath. Chris knew to wait for her, but with the added responsibility of Sara's daughter, not to mention a nut on the loose; Annie didn't want to be late. She stood back out of the way and kept a close watch on the school doors. A warm feeling of contentment flowed through her body. Crazy, considering the day she'd just been through. But she loved this; the air of expectancy, waiting to see her child's beautiful face after a day apart. Then bam, the doors flew open and a hundred kids wrapped up in a rainbow of colors spilled out laughing and talking without a worry in the world. Some of the older children headed off down the walk in groups of four and five while the younger ones searched anxiously for their parents. Then big beams of joy lit little faces as they ran into hugs and smiles from their loved ones.

Then it was Annie's turn. Chris and Jessica burst out of the little crowd surrounding them and hurried towards her, waving good-bye over their shoulders to their friends.

"Mom, guess what?"

"Annie, my tooth is loose. Wanna see?" Jessica opened her mouth and wiggled her front tooth with her tongue.

"You told. You said I could tell her." Chris pouted.

"Okay, it doesn't matter who tells me, does it?" Annie crouched down between the two of them. "Let's see that again, Jess." She grabbed her son's hand and squeezed. Jessica happily obliged. Her little mouth popped open like a bird's and her tongue pushed through the gap, the tooth laid almost right over. "Holy moly, it's loose all right.

I'll give you an apple when we get home and it'll probably pop right out. Then you get to put the tooth under your pillow for the tooth fairy to exchange for money."

Two sets of eyes grew large. Chris leaned closer to get a better look. "She's going to have a hole in her mouth," he stated triumphantly, pointing to the gap.

"It's only temporary. A new adult tooth will come up in its spot." Annie smiled when Jess stood taller at her statement. "Okay kids, time to go home." They skipped over to their bikes chattering about whether or not they'd see the fairy when she came. Chris got his bike unlocked first and backed it out of the rack before pushing it up for her to hold while he put his helmet on.

"Mom, when can I get adult teeth?" His wistful green eyes gazed up at her as if she could solve the world.

Annie's heart clenched a little at the mention of adult anything in relation to her son. He was her baby. While she loved watching him take the steps toward manhood, she was in no hurry for him to arrive there.

"Your turn will come, son." Then, seeing his crestfallen expression, "Girls lose theirs sooner because we're smaller. Boys grow big and strong, so their teeth need longer to mature." He sighed, but seemed to accept her explanation. She leaned down to give him a hug. "You're my big boy. I bet the tooth fairy can't wait until it's your turn. She'll get a nice white, healthy tooth from you for her collection." Finally, a real smile. She hated to see her son upset, even though sometimes it couldn't be helped.

Jessica pulled up beside them, helmet in place, a *Frozen* backpack nestled against her spine. "And we're off." The kids released a war-whoop and took off, racing for the curb at the end of the block where they knew to stop and wait. Annie followed at a leisurely pace, not in any kind of rush to return to work. The trees had lost most of their foliage in the last few days. The walkways were littered with a multi-hued collection of leaves. She loved this time of year; the crispness of the air, the almost startling brightness of the blue sky, and best of all, the brilliant reds and oranges of the Maple trees.

Her thoughts returned to today's events, and Jared. She was glad he'd been there, he'd made the traumatic morning easier to bear. For a couple of brief moments the awkwardness and anger had disappeared and they'd been friends again. Annie missed that. She missed him. So much. She had plenty of women to go out with, chat with, but it wasn't the same. Something between her and Jared just clicked. Always had. Even back in the early days when he stood up for her against the bullies in school. It had always been Jared and Annie against the world. Then he left.

Her pace kicked up a notch until she caught up to the kids. "Good job waiting, you guys. I was thinking—Jessica's loose tooth deserves a celebration. How about stopping at Grace's for a dish of ice cream?"

The sun had nothing on the children's smiles at the mention of their favorite treat. "Yay, I want chocolate." Chris immediately decided.

Jessica took a few moments longer, mulling over her choices. "I think I would like strawberry." Then, as if remembering her mother's warning in her head, she tacked on, "Please."

Annie's insides filled with gooey warmth for the two little munchkins. "You bet, sweetie. Okay then, let's see who makes it first to the end of the next block."

Jared's world narrowed down to the little black barrel of the gun pointed at his chest. Funny, in all the years of being in the SEAL teams he'd never been in this situation. Not to say he hadn't dodged his share of bullets. It's just they'd always erupted like a hailstorm, out of nowhere. This was somewhere. The back alley of his mother's freaking café in freaking America to be exact. *What the hell?*

If he wasn't so pissed off at himself for getting into this situation, he might have laughed. Eight years overseas off and on, and he was going to get shot in his own backyard. How's that for ironic?

"Look man, why don't we talk about this?" Jared forced his gaze to focus on Sergei's steely gaze instead of the muzzle of the semi-automatic.

"The time for talk is past," the Russian said. "You ignored my advice and instead made a fool out of me with that stupid trick you performed."

"Advice? You call beating the livin' shit out of me, advice?" Jared ground his teeth together, and fought to keep a level tone. "You can't blame a guy for wanting to retaliate." A crash by the garbage caused both men to crouch into a fight stance. A tabby cat raced away. Jared straightened, his heart knocking against his ribcage, as desperate to escape this mess as the animal. He needed to defuse the situation before someone came upon them; please God not his mom.

"Okay, you're right. I shouldn't have set off alarms or caused those slots to pay out. But seriously dude, you can't go around acting all KGB, we're in the good old USA now." Jared kept a careful eye on the guy's trigger finger and cursed his loose tongue. What part of defuse couldn't he figure out?

Sergei tipped his felt hat back on his bald head like an old time gunslinger. His hand holding the gun never wavered. "You have big mouth."

Yeah, I've heard that a time or ten.

"Why don't we handle this like two adults? I'll call your boss, tell him I screwed up and it'll never happen again..." There was no doubt on that, if he ever went near a casino again he'd kick his own ass. "And then you can go back to ruling your little kingdom far, far, away."

Click.

The sound of the hammer cocking reverberated with frightening clarity in the small alley. There wasn't even anywhere for him to take cover. The garbage can was at least ten feet away. Jared's jaw cramped from the tension. His skin crawled as if overrun with fire ants. Where was his team when he needed them?

He'd just decided the only alternative was to rush the son-of-a-bitch when the alley erupted with the screams and laughter of children. Two kids rounded the corner at full speed on pedal bikes, racing each other to an imaginary finish line.

Fuck.

Sergei seized the opportunity, stepped between the bicycles and scooped the kids off their seats. The bikes, wheels still turning, fell to the ground in front of him creating a barrier. The kids—God, it was Chris and little Jessica—shrieked until Sergei shook them, then they froze, eyes wide and frightened, hanging under his arms like rag dolls.

"Let them go, you motherfu..." Jared's voice came out low and lethal. Every muscle in his body prepared itself for the moment of attack. His breathing slowed until he could count each heartbeat as the blood coursed through his veins. Waiting. Watching.

Barnikov laughed. Laughed. The prick.

"Now it my turn to play game." Jared made a slight move and Sergei's smile flat-lined. He dropped Jessica to the ground in front of him but kept his forearm wrapped around her neck. The gun nestled the side of her head pointed straight at Chris dangling from his other arm. "Move and I shoot." He shuffled the trio back towards the mouth of the alley. "We'll talk again, my friend."

And then he disappeared around the corner, leaving nothing but the slowly turning tire on a bike and Jared's heart as it shattered.

CHAPTER FIFTEEN

Jared jumped over the discarded bikes in the dim alley and ran for the corner, his breath suspended in his throat and heart pounding *No, No, No.* How had this happened? What could he tell Annie? Nick and Sara?

Where did the fucker go?

His feet almost skidded out from under him when he rounded the building. His head swung left to right in a frantic search of the empty street, but no one was there. Not even any witnesses. *Stupid, damn one horse town.* Dusk, and the freaking streets rolled up for the night. *Help.* He needed help. Now.

He drew out his cell and hit one on the keypad as he raced down the walk, his gaze peeled for anything suspicious.

Three interminable rings later the chief picked up. "Yeah?"

"I need you, man. Hurry." Now the air sawed in and out of Jared's lungs so hard he could barely speak.

"Jared?" Frank's tone turned sharp. "What the hell's going on? Where are you?"

Where were they? The slam of a trunk across the street drew his gaze. There. He caught a glint of chrome when a car door opened in a tree-lined driveway. A shadowy figure climbed behind the wheel. Jared dropped the phone and ran.

The engine screamed to life and the car roared onto the road with no lights, narrowly missing him as he jumped out of its path. It took off down the street and Jared gave chase until long after it disappeared from view. He stumbled to a halt and stood breathing harsh, hands braced on his knees and head hanging low, gaze focused on the inky darkness descending like a shroud of doom.

When he could no longer hear the fading rumble of the motor, he turned and made his way back to the tinny roar of Frank's voice coming through his phone.

"Talk to me, Martin. So help me God, if you don't answer..."

"They're gone, Chief." Jared hated even putting voice to the words. "That dirty mother-fucker took them and I couldn't stop him." Defeat and self-loathing turned his stomach inside out. He swiped a shaky hand down his face and smacked his thigh. "What am I going to do?"

"First, tell me what the hell is going on. Then call the local PD and tell them what you told me, understand?"

The impact of what had just happened hit him. He sunk to his knees, right there in the middle of the empty street. Lights had blinked on in the nearby homes. He could see families sitting down together for dinner, smiling, chatting, without a worry in the world.

"Did I tell you I have a son, Frank?" Jared kept his gaze focused on those happy families and slowly the ache in his chest turned to rage and retribution. "I have a son. That bastard Sergei Barnikov just signed his own death warrant. I gotta go, Chief." He slammed the phone shut, jumped to his feet, turned toward the cop shop, and froze.

Annie faced him, fist pressed against her mouth. Her eyes shone with despair while tears streamed down her face. She stared at him with denial.

Fear.

Dread.

The fist lowered, reached for him. His feet unglued, and he hurried the last few steps to her side, grasping her cold hand. "Annie, I'm so sorry. I tried to stop him. I really did."

"We were on our way to have some ice cream. I told the kids to put their bikes around back and meet me at Grace's," she whispered, all but shrinking before him. Jared gently pulled her into his arms and just held on. She resisted at first, then gave in. Her head nestled against his heart seeking solace as she leaned into him. "Why didn't I follow them, Jared? I should have followed them." She began to cry in earnest, big racking sobs that shook her whole body and soaked his shirt.

Helpless, Jared ran his hands up and down her spine. When the tears slowed somewhat he cradled her head and tipped it back so she'd look at him. Tears ravaged her face, bathed with light from the streetlamps. It broke his heart. He placed a gentle kiss upon her forehead. "Honey, it's not your fault. Please, Annie, none of this is your fault, okay? Don't blame yourself. If you want to hate someone, I'm the one who brought that pig to town, hate me."

"Who is he, Jared? What does he want? Why did he take my babies?" Her voice rose with each question as panic set in. "How are we going to find them? God, what if he hurts them?"

He wished he had a positive answer to give her. He didn't. Truth was, he had no idea what the Russian had planned. Best-case scenario would be ransom, or a swap. His worthless hide for the children's. But he just didn't know.

"C'mon honey, let's head over to the police station. Maybe your friend Jack can help." Right now Jared would take anyone's offer of assistance.

Annie pulled away and rubbed her face on her sleeve before straightening her clothes. They moved quietly down the street for a few moments. "You know, don't you?" she asked with a brief sideways glance, before turning her gaze back to the path they were taking.

Her words caused the last of his doubts to fade along with the anger and betrayal. "Yeah, I know." He halted their progress and waited until she faced him. "He's a beautiful little boy, Annie. We need to talk about this. Soon. But for right now, let's just worry about getting them back safe and sound, okay?"

Annie sniffled and continued down the street, but not before she closed the distance between them and slid her fingers around his. Jared's heart squeezed back.

Frank Stein swore, pocketed his cell, then grabbed up the reins of his horse and wheeled toward the ranch, squinting against the late Texas sun. He'd fought against the premonition he'd had for the past week. His abuela would have been proud. At least now he knew where it was coming from. He'd have to get next week's payroll done, talk to Spencer about moving the cattle down from the hills, and make sure his mother would be okay while he helped out Jared.

In their decade long friendship Frank had never heard his friend sound quite so desperate. Jared had a talent for getting himself into trouble, but except for last spring when Frank had to fly to Vegas and bail him out of jail, he'd always managed to come out smelling like a rose. Still, if his buddy needed him, he'd be there, like yesterday. The ranch would be fine in his foreman's more than capable hands. Now that Spencer was dating his mom, Frank didn't need to worry so much about her anymore.

All of which left him too much time to think about the beautiful DEA agent he'd had an altercation with while in Vegas, Magdalena Holt. Maggie.

His mouth quirked, knowing what she'd say to him calling her by her full name. It was the way he thought of her though, fierce and fiery. The first time he'd seen her, she'd made a lasting impression. She'd been working a case and had arrived dressed for undercover work as a prostitute to question him before Jared's release. Maggie had flat-out bowled him over and she hadn't been far from his mind ever since. And then there was the interesting fact that her partner just happened to be one of Frank's men long thought dead...speaking of complicated.

The horse brushed through thorny mesquite bushes and he inhaled the sweet scent. His home. Frank felt the weight of responsibility as his gaze scanned the horizon. Every square mile in any direction belonged to their family, had for generations. He took his duty seriously. Knew it was up to him to preserve it for Stein's to come. His brother, Cameron had loved the land, often staying out for days among the snakes and coyotes. When he'd first gone missing everyone thought that's what he'd been doing, but Frank had known different. That damn sixth sense of his was more often a curse than a blessing. His abuela had told him often not to take such a precious gift for granted, but he hated the knowledge. Every time it came upon him, something bad happened to someone he cared about.

Maybe if the dreams were more fully formed so that he could do something to change what might happen. But no, his *gift* came with boundaries. All he could do is wait and watch and pray. Not that it had helped either his father or his brother, but hey, you never know, maybe one day.

His saddle creaked as he leaned over to give the bay a pat on the neck. The horse was one of his favorites, sure-footed and calm, they'd been through some bad storms together. "Another hour, Sadie, and then you can enjoy a nice rub down and maybe some oats, how's that sound?" Her ears flicked back, listening to the soothing cadence of his voice. Out in the hills a man tended to share a lot with his horse. They developed a level of trust in each other's survival he didn't often see.

Except in the teams.

Just between him and Sadie, he missed the comradery and excitement. He even missed the freaking tasteless MRE's. But most of all he missed his men. Nick, his point man who'd gone and found himself a new family in Tidal Falls. Adam, who far from dead as they'd all believed, was now a high-ranking DEA agent with Maggie Holt. And then there was Jared, his right-hand man and best friend. To look at the guy with his laid-back attitude and tattooed body you'd never know he was a near genius, especially with electronics. There wasn't much he couldn't do with wires or computers, all of which made him invaluable on their missions. But also tended to land him in shit. He'd get bored, start playing around, and next thing you know they were dodging bullets. Frank smiled, the good old days.

The ranch house came into sight nestled against the foothills, safe against the ferocious winter winds and fierce summer heat. They loved the old place, him and his mother, even though it was too big for the two of them. A rambling white structure with obvious additions added in the past, it was a part of the land surrounding it. A wraparound deck finished the haphazard look, perfect to sit and enjoy a beer in the evening and listen to the cicadas chirp. The outbuildings formed a distant safe circle around the compound. Sheds, barns, housing, they even had their own general store. He treasured his home, and hated it all at the same time. There was always something that needed doing, whether it be the books, feeding and managing livestock, planting crops, preparing for winter, the list oftentimes felt endless. But he'd never give it up. There was immense pride to be felt at the end of a long, hard day of driving steers when he could stand back and gaze at heads of fat, healthy cattle on their way to market. He only wished Cam were here to share it with him.

Frank rode down into the yard and pulled up before the barn. He'd just stepped from the saddle when Spencer came ambling out of the cow shed.

"'Bout time you got yourself back here, was beginning to think we'd need a posse to track you down," he grumbled, and spat a wad of chewing tobacco out the side of his mouth.

Frank peeled his leather gloves off, smacked them against his thigh and shoved them in his back pocket. "I told you I had to check the east pasture, old man. It's a full day's ride there and back."

Spencer shoved his worn cowboy hat back on his head. "Sure, 'n I know that. Tell your ma. She's been pestering me all day." He shook his head and scratched his grizzled whiskers. "She kept mumbling something about you leaving. I tried to tell her you'd be back, but…"

Frank wasn't surprised his mom knew he had to go away for a while. She always did. They shared the same prescience, passed down from generation to generation. He'd learned not to question it, and actually in times of stress the foresight brought a measure of peace. Such as in the case of Cameron's disappearance. Even though many thought him dead, Frank and his mom knew better. He was alive. They didn't know where, or why he stayed away, but at least they shared the faith they would see him again one day.

"I'll go in and talk to her. Can you watch the ranch for a few days?" He rubbed a tired hand across the back of his neck. "Jared called today."

Spencer grinned, his teeth browned from the tobacco. "What that boy go and do this time?"

"Don't know, but I need to go. He'd do it for me."

Frank took up Sadie's reins and led her into the barn to her stall. The other horses nickered soft greetings as he stripped her saddle and blanket and gave her a thorough rubdown, her skin twitching with pleasure. Spencer entered the stall with a bucket of oats and armful of hay for her feeder sending dust motes flying into the air, and nudged her out of his way.

"Hold on there, missy. Give me half a minute." Spencer dropped the food and Sadie chuffed with contentment. The two men worked together to brush her to a shine, the swish of her tail and chomping filling the comfortable silence.

"How long will you be gone?" Spencer asked from his spot near Sadie's withers, his gnarled old hand straightening her mane.

"Not long, I hope. Busy time here, I can't afford to be gone long." Frank said, his mind already working out the logistics of his trip. He'd have to call Jared back and find out exactly where he was flying to, maybe get a better sense of the situation after his friend had calmed down a little.

"You should be okay. We hired those new wranglers last month. They're working out well, so I think you'll be good for manpower." Frank's forehead creased as he considered the best way to bring up his more immediate concern. "Listen, I ah...I don't want Mom left in the big house alone. Maybe you could stay up there with her?" He hurried to tack on, "in a guest room, of course." No way was he entertaining the notion of what his mom might, or might not do in the sanctuary of her own bedroom.

Spencer cackled, the old coot. Frank glared; *glad he thinks this is funny.*

"Take your time, your mom and I will be just fine. This ranch plumb runs itself. Don't you be worrying none about us." Spence winked.

Frank snorted, just what he needed, a couple of frisky old-timers. "Yeah well, just make sure you check on those heifers we have in the cow barn. They should be dropping any time now."

Spencer straightened and poked his chin out, full of injured pride. "Don't you be trying to tell me how to run this here place. Me and your dad done taught you, and don't you damn forget it."

Remorse hit Frank right between the eyes. Just because he was a bit embarrassed talking about his mother's love life, he had no business coming down hard on Spencer. He didn't think they'd still have a farm to run without the other man. Spencer had been the glue that held them all together when first Frank's father died in a freak accident, and then his brother later disappeared. Emily, his mother, had blamed herself for not noticing her youngest son's despair and slumped into depression after he vanished. It was only with Spencer's continued persistence that she finally pulled herself back and found a new happiness with the ranch foreman. Frank was happy for them. He just didn't want to dwell on the details, that's all.

"Sorry. Guess I'm just worried about Jared. I'm going to head up to the house, you coming for supper?" He offered as a peace offering of sorts.

"Nah, I'll let you two chaw tonight. I imagine you'll be gone by daybreak?"

Frank nodded.

Spencer cleared his throat and tipped his hat over his eyes. "Take care of yourself, boy."

Frank swallowed a hard lump of regret. "Yeah, I will." He left his old friend sweeping the stable and trudged across the yard to the welcoming glow of home.

CHAPTER SIXTEEN

Exasperated, Jared pushed away from the sheriff's freakishly neat desk, his chair scraping backward on the yellowed linoleum. "I've already told you everything I know. Twice." He ignored Annie's warning frown and rose to pace the room. "None of this is getting those kids home."

"Jared..."

"No thanks to you." Jack spoke over Annie, his gaze flickering to Jared then back onto the computer screen as his finger plunked at the keyboard. "We're doing everything we can. I have an all-points bulletin out for the missing car, and a description of both the suspect and the kids..." Annie choked back a sob and he reached for her hand. "We'll find them."

Jared snorted. He couldn't help it. He'd never felt so frustrated, so helpless. He needed to be out there looking, not sitting on his laurels going over useless details. In the rational corner of his mind he knew this was necessary, crucial to the recovery effort, but he didn't feel too sane right now. They'd been here for hours. Dawn's rays pushed through the grey blinds, and still they'd heard nothing. *Where is that son-of-a-bitch?*

What kind of a person steals children? The answer to that made him gag. He'd seen how depraved humans could treat each other firsthand. Please, not that. Let this all end well. He'd gladly turn himself over to the Russian, if only the kids could be safe. Please, God.

Annie stared vacantly into space, her eyes sunken with dark rings on pale tear-streaked cheeks. He needed to get her home for some rest. She'd need her strength later when they found Chris and Jessica. He breathed out a silent curse and moved to crouch by her side.

"Honey, you need to go home and get some sleep. You're not going to do anyone any good if you don't rest."

His heart hurt as she gazed down at him with hopeless, lackluster eyes. "Where are they, Jared? I want my baby. What is he doing to my child?" The desolation in her voice tore him apart.

"Sergei Barnikov is playing a game. It's me he wants." Jared squeezed her knee through her jeans. "Don't worry, he won't hurt those kids, they're his guarantee. He messes that up, he has nothing."

Jack leaned back and crossed his thick arms. "And what makes you so damn important that a highly regarded business man from Las Vegas would come to *our* town and commit such a barbaric act?"

Jared surged to his feet, anger bleeding out of every pore, but then the sight of the sheriff rubbing a hand over a tired, bristly face stemmed the tide. He sighed, this wasn't getting them anywhere. "I don't know what his motive is. I admit I screwed up a while ago, but I've also paid the price. This makes no more sense to me than it does to you, Jack."

The sound of his name seemed to loosen the starch out of the sheriff's attitude. Jack's gaze moved to Annie and turned soft and sad. He cleared his throat and stood, shuffling a few perfectly stacked papers into another impeccable mound. "Listen, I'm going to stay here and work on this. Why don't you let Jared take you home and get some sleep?" Then, before she could voice the protest forming on her lips, he added, "I'll call the second I hear anything, I promise."

Annie shook her head, but then realizing the wisdom of his words, her shoulders slumped and she sighed. "Okay, you're right. I won't be able to sleep, but I'd better get some rest. Chris will want to talk my ear off if he..." She choked up and looked down at her wringing hands.

Jared reached down to gently pull Annie to her feet. When she was head to chest with him, he tipped her chin up until he could look into the fern green depths of her eyes. "When—not if— when. I promise, okay?"

After a long drawn out moment, she gave a slow nod of assent. "Okay."

Sergei glanced into the rearview mirror for the tenth time, studiously ignoring the frightened gazes of the children. He'd warned them to keep quiet or he'd lock them in the trunk. They'd listened. The road remained dark and quiet. He'd taken the first country lane he came across and travelled until he hit a crossroads, then turned right. The further away from town he drove, the more sparse the homes, which suited him fine.

He'd promised Chenglei some prime specimens for his upcoming sale and now he could provide them. The sour taste in his mouth would fade. He had to remember this was about getting his honor back. Nothing else could matter. Not even two little children with eyes that reminded him of his own many years ago.

"Where are you taking us, mister?" It was the boy. His young voice shook with fear.

Sergei jerked and looked over his shoulder, his attention diverted from the dark path he followed with only a hide-and-seek moon for light. The kid had freaky eyes. They spooked him, and were weirdly familiar. Thoughts flitted back and forth like the fireflies beyond his window. Martin's best friend, the craft store owner. Or maybe she was much more? Suddenly it all made perfect sense and he burst out laughing, startling the kids in back.

"What's so funny?" The little girl asked with a defiant tone.

"Life. Life is funny," he answered. "You two sit back and keep your mouths shut or you won't like the consequences." He watched them look at each other, then slouch in their seats. Maybe Chenglei would have to wait after all.

Annie looked up at Jared standing in front of her in Jack's sterile office and wondered how they'd arrived at this place in their lives. She'd been in love with this man for nearly half her life, yet he'd never known. And now they were here, fighting to get their child back. Fate was a funny thing. Suddenly she had the overwhelming urge to tell him everything. How much that night had meant to her. The crazy foods she'd eaten while pregnant. The immediate adoration when the doctor placed her squalling, red-faced son in her arms. How many times she'd picked up the phone to call him, only to set it down again. All the nights spent dreaming of him, of them. To ask him what happened. Where had they gone so wrong?

The clearing of a throat made her blink, and her gaze refocused on the room instead of the past. She turned away from the concern apparent in Jared's watchful eyes to face Jack, her white knight. Why couldn't she have fallen in love with him? Steady, loyal, strong. Not someone to run when things get tough. In other words, perfect.

But, he wasn't Jared.

Jack looked as tired as she felt. Annie knew he'd spent all day yesterday working on her break-in, then all night on...she gulped back a fresh onslaught of tears, they wouldn't bring her son back. She needed to go home, re-group, and come back fighting. The kids needed her.

"Thanks, Jack—for everything. I'll be back in a couple of hours. Please, please call if you hear anything at all." His head dipped in agreement, a solitary man standing there on the other side of the desk. Annie brushed past Jared, scowling at the flash of awareness she couldn't control. She wished she felt more than fondness as she gazed into Jack's endearing face. But now that Jared had returned she knew it wasn't fair; it was time to end their dating relationship.

"I'm sorry, Jack." Her words were husky and filled with regret.

His eyes filled with sad acceptance, he reached out and cupped her cheek before leaning down to give her a soft good-bye kiss. "Me too, sweetheart." He held her for another moment before letting his hand fall and stepping back. "Okay, get going. I have a lot of work to do here and you're interrupting my flow." He gave her a lop-sided grin to show her no hard feelings.

Shaky fingers swiped away the tears and she smiled back, then turned for the door, surprised to find Jared hot on her heels.

"I can find my own way home, you know," she sniped.

"Humor me. I don't want you walking alone." He held the door open with an arm above her head, too close for comfort.

She shrugged in annoyance and stomped through the opening. "Well, come on then. I don't want to take all day."

"Yes, ma'am."

The teasing smile in his voice only made her walk faster. She couldn't wait to get home and slam the door on the whole human race. Annie squinted in the early morning sun; surprised to see the world had carried on without her. It felt as if everything that happened in the last few hours was a bad dream she couldn't break free of. Even in the early days after her father left and her mother took out her hurt in pills and alcohol, Annie had always managed to find that ray of light to give her the strength to carry on.

Not now.

Though the sun shone bright in her face, loss and sorrow blinded her. Chris would be so scared. He was his mommy's boy, and she loved him with every fiber of her being. Too late, she understood what drove her own mom to react the way she had. Desperation gave wings to her feet, and soon she was full out running down the walk, her breaths deep gasps of agonized pain.

"Annie...Annie slow down. You're going to hurt yourself." Jared jogged at her side, his eyes worried. "C'mon baby, this won't help anyone. Please, Annie."

She ignored him and kept up her pace for a couple more blocks before slowing down when they got to her street. How could she walk through that door, see Chris's toys? His room? "I can't go in there." Her deepest fear poured out, the words scraping her throat with their sharp edges. "What if he doesn't come back?"

Jared was a grim presence at her side, as if he too didn't want to face that possibility. "He has to come back. I can't accept anything less."

She realized all she'd deprived him of by not making those calls. His son. His beautiful baby boy. "I'm sorry I never told you, Jared. You're right, you had a right to know." She hesitated, not sure how to explain her reasons. "At first it was because I was hurt..."

He jerked, then swung her around to face him. "Did I hurt you that night? God, Annie I'm an idiot. I knew you were innocent and yet I attacked you anyway. I'm the one who's sorry." He tried to tug her into his arms, but she had to make him understand first.

"You're wrong. Oh, I was *innocent* as you put it, but you never did anything I wasn't craving you to do for years. Do you hear me, Jared? Years. I waited and waited for you to notice me, but you never did." She pushed against the rock wall of his chest in frustration. "I was always the best bud. The one you came to about your girlfriend problems." He winced and she quieted, "The one you shared your disappointments and dreams with. And all I ever wanted was for you to really *see me*." The last came out under her breath as she let herself fold into his warm hold. "To see how much I loved you." His heart beneath her ear beat with the force of a thousand drums. His arms tightened until he lifted her clear off her feet, before slowly loosening his grasp so she could slide back down to earth.

He used one hand to tip her chin up and what she saw in his eyes caused her heart to join the riot. Love. The emotion pouring out of his beautiful blue-green depths and shining from behind the lens of his glasses—was love. *Holy cow.*

"I never thought I'd hear you say those words. Jesus, Annie, you know how to bring a man to his knees. Come 'ere." He leaned down and then there he was, those masculine, sexy, to dream for, lips, were on hers.

Shock made her still for a couple of wasted seconds. Then, *oh my God*, those lips were moving and she was losing her mind because nothing had ever felt so good, or so right. Her arms slid up around his neck to anchor her body. Her fingers slid into the crisp ends of his hair and it was just as she remembered, except better somehow. His chest, his thighs, and the growing hardness she could feel against her stomach, all so real. Not a dream then.

A horn tooted behind them, jarring her out of the moment. Annie jumped back in time to see the curious smile from Rebecca as she drove by on her way to school. She'd have to call and let them know Chris and Jessica wouldn't be in today. And just like that everything came rushing back. What was she doing standing on a street corner kissing when her little boy was in the hands of a madman? This proved it, she was certifiable. Disgusted, she turned and headed up her walk, hoping Jared would take a hint and leave. He didn't.

"Annie, c'mon, we didn't do anything wrong." She could hear the scuff of his boots as he followed her and sighed. She wasn't up to having this conversation right now.

"Did you get hold of Nick yet? I tried Sara again, but received no answer." She kept her focus on the key she'd placed in the lock.

"No, I think they're up-island, shitty cell service. Jack called the RCMP, they'll get word to them." He stood so close, his voice rumbled through her back from his chest. A leanly muscled, richly tattooed arm reached around and his hand closed over hers on the key. "Let me help you, Annie. Let's do this together, you and me, okay?"

She had the urge to simply lean back and let him take control. She was tired of being the responsible one. The boring one. In a corner of her mind, Annie always wondered what if. What if she'd grown up beautiful and sexy, instead of steadfast and smart? What if her parents hadn't died, or Jared deserted her. What if.

But she knew the answer to that. If she hadn't learned to be reliable and book savvy, her business wouldn't be doing as well as it did. If her parents were still around she may not have found her independence, or had her son. And if Jared hadn't left...well, that was a dream she'd buried deep years ago. Right now though, as she prepared to open the door on the remnants of the children's rush to leave for school yesterday morning, she was thankful not to have to do it alone.

Her head dipped in silent acknowledgement and then they were in the door, facing a home left in limbo. Chris's rubber boots flopped over in the entry, his spare jacket that she'd asked him to hang up at least ten times, stacked on top. Jessica's doll sat patiently waiting on the sofa facing the door. Chris's latest *Lego* project lay discarded on her coffee table. The worst though, the silence. Her house was rarely silent. Not with an active little boy who loved to dress up as different super heroes and save the world, or an evil villain with magical powers no one could destroy.

Annie let her own coat and purse fall beside that of her son's, her throat tight with unshed tears. She forced herself to tread toward the kitchen and the promise of fortifying coffee. She glanced back to ask Jared if he still took it black, and slowed to a stop. Annie knew this would be hard for her, but she hadn't considered how he would feel. He was getting a glimpse into his son's world for the very first time, and his wonder and pain were obvious. His face wore an expression of regret as he lifted Chris's jacket, so small in his father's big hands, and straightened the inside-out sleeves before gently hanging it on the lower hook. Her heart cried with him as his gaze took in the blocks, the sword, the life of his child he'd never been a part of, the life he'd missed. The famous words, *Oh, what a tangled web we weave*, by Sir Walter Scott, jumped into her head. It had never been truer.

The only solution was to move forward. There's nothing she could do about past mistakes, but she could certainly make sure the future was different. Jared would know his son. He would have the opportunity to take Chris to ball games, go fishing together, guide him in learning to drive, and even about girls.

If Chris came home.

Needing to keep busy, Annie turned away. Though she was far from hungry, she left Jared to his own devices and strode into the kitchen to make them something to eat. Soon the house took on the welcoming scents of maple bacon, toast, and fresh brewed dark roast coffee. She'd just finished making them each a sandwich when Jared wandered into the room.

"Mm, something smells good," he said, making an obvious play for normalcy. "Is there something I can do?"

"No, grab a seat. I'll bring it over." Annie nodded to the kitchen table in the corner of the room, before turning back to the counter to grab the mugs. She needed to give herself a moment to get used to the fact Jared was in her home. She carried the cups over, sat them down, and hurried back for the sandwich plates. When she returned to the table it was to see Jared gazing down at Chris's art project he'd forgotten to take to school. He'd made a painting of the ocean, a pod of three killer whales jumping high above multi-colored waves. Anything he lacked in technique was more than made up for in spirit.

"This is pretty good. Chris?" Jared glanced up at her, his fingers tracing the print.

"Yes, he was supposed to turn it in yesterday, but as you can see..."

"Late," Jared smiled. "I remember those days. Ma telling me to get it done or I'd be in big trouble when Dad got home." They stared at each other awkwardly for a moment before Annie sat down and pushed his plate toward him.

"Eat, before it gets cold. Do you take anything in your coffee?"

"No, strong and black. This smells perfect, thanks."

They were almost done their meal when an old tortoise colored tabby cat wandered in and jumped onto the chair beside them.

"Someone smelled the food," Jared said and pulled off a piece of bacon to feed to the animal looking at him with haughty disdain.

"Fitzroy, get down, you know better." Annie tried to wave him away, and was promptly ignored.

Jared eyed her in surprise. "No way. Is this the same Fitzroy I gave you as a kitten?"

He could have added, the night before he left town for eight years. The night they made soul-destroying love and then he walked away. The night she'd thought they were finally, finally after years of unreciprocated adoration, going to be a couple. The night her dreams died. Yeah, that night.

"Yep, that's him all right. About twenty pounds heavier and eight years older." She reached over and gave her cat a rub behind the ears, smiling when his diesel engine purr began and he leaned into her touch. She glanced up and caught a bemused look on Jared's face. "What? You didn't think I'd keep him after you took off? I'm not the one to ignore my responsibilities, that's your department." Good to know she wasn't bitter or anything. She grimaced and got up to place the plates in the sink, but Jared snagged her wrist. Annie turned angry eyes from her captured arm to his face, "Let me go." Her harsh tone sent the cat scurrying away.

"No. Not until we talk this out. It's gone on long enough, don't you think?"

She frowned at the hypercritical tone he took and tried to pull away, but he wouldn't let go. "Only about eight years too long, yes. If you hadn't turned tail and run the next day after we did..." she waved a frustrated hand between them, "you know, we might have had a chance of saving our friendship. Now, I'm not so sure. Maybe it's too late for us, Jared." Her stomach dropped at the thought.

He lifted her bound hand and tugged. She squeaked and landed sideways in his lap with his arms wrapped snug around her ribs. "This is better, now we can talk." He leaned in and kissed her nose. "You always did have a red-head's temper." And then, before she could do more than sputter, his mouth was on hers, and she forgot to breathe.

His wickedly mobile lips were everywhere at once, the corner of her mouth, her jaw, her ear. Annie whimpered, needing more, needing everything. She was going up in flames with just his kisses, what would it feel like to know his body again? Her hands roamed up and down his rugged forearms. She tipped her head back to grant him access to her throat. He latched onto her breast and even through her shirt the suction bowed her back. He stood and started down the hall, her still in his arms, his voice a guttural command, "Which way?"

Annie hesitated. This was the wrong time. Her focus should be on how to get her child back, not in her own selfish pleasure. But she needed Jared's heat to warm her soul-deep fear.

Maybe he needed her too.

"There, first door on the left."

CHAPTER SEVENTEEN

Maggie woke to a chorus of moans and groans. Hers. Everything ached, from her toes to the follicles of hair on her head. From the little she could see out of her swollen lids, they'd moved her. The shadowy image of bars and the cold cement floor beneath her face told her she was in some sort of cage. Her nose crinkled against the stench of urine and who knows what else.

She tried to roll onto her side and get a better view of the room, but gasped in agony. Her ribs were either cracked or broken. It made breathing a bitch. A faint sound in the corner jerked her gaze around, her heart pounding like a run-away horse. There, the outline of a body propped against the wall, head of blond hair hanging low. Olga, it had to be. Relief swept through her, she'd thought the other woman was dead. When the guards broke through the flimsy barrier barring the door of their previous prison, Maggie fought with everything she had to stop them from rushing for the window.

All the women escaped. Except Olga. She'd given up her freedom to give the others a chance. The men had grabbed both of them with brutal hands and forced them down the hall to Chenglei.

Maggie thought they would be killed then and there, but apparently he planned to toy with them for a while first.

"Olga," her voice was little more than a whisper, paper thin and dry. She coughed and almost blacked out from the discomfort. It took her a while to get up the courage to try again. This time she wrapped an aching arm around her ribcage for support first. "Olga, talk to me. How bad are you injured?"

At first there was no movement, then slowly the other woman's head lifted, lank hair falling to the side. Maggie gasped. Olga's eyelids were purple and black and swollen completely shut. Her lips were caricatures of a bad lipo commercial, but the worst was her left cheekbone. It sat grotesquely higher than the right, and the skin underneath where her cheek should be located sagged in a rainbow of color. The collarbone on the same side poked almost through the skin, obviously broken, and her arm hung awkwardly at her side.

"Oh, Olga. I'm so sorry. Those bastards." Maggie's stomach rolled at the viciousness of the attack. She'd spent the last fifteen months undercover alongside some of the worst scum on Las Vegas streets and thought she'd seen it all, but this was the worst. If she didn't get them out of here soon, Olga wouldn't survive. Maggie gathered her strength, then with a mighty heave, she braced and rolled onto her hands and knees, gasping at the sharp pinch in her chest and back. Again, she lost track of time, all her focus on the pain roaring through her body like a freight train. When the dirty floor finally came into view through her blurry, tear-filled vision, she made her way, inch, by painstaking inch, across the room until she collapsed at Olga's bare feet.

Frustration ate at Adam O'Connor like a cancer. He slammed the agency car door and sprinted through the drizzling rain for the stairs of Vancouver General Hospital. A local farmer had found six women naked, bruised, and bloody when he entered his barn to begin his day's chores. He'd called 911 and an emergency response team rushed to the site. So far as Adam knew, there were no signs of sexual assault, but the women were dehydrated, malnourished, and weak. As soon as he heard about the case, he booked a trip to Canada, and prayed this was the break he'd been waiting for.

A quick stop at reception sent him to the trauma wing. His Oxford's squeaked on the shiny tile flooring as he made his way down a seemingly endless corridor to the room of his first witness, fifteen-year-old Sandra Tate. He flashed his badge to the officer guarding the door before taking a deep breath and entering. The first thing he noticed was the sterile smell of antiseptic and the beep, beep, beep of the machines feeding the gaunt body in the narrow hospital bed. A tired looking couple hunched over their sleeping daughter. Upon hearing the door swoosh open they glanced around, and fear changed to anger.

"Why didn't you people find her before this could happen?" Mrs. Tate cried, her body shaking with the force of her pain. Her husband laid calming hands over her shoulders, his eyes haunted.

"Hush, Mary, you know the police were doing their best. We have her back now, that's what counts." He bent over and kissed his wife's prematurely grey head.

"I'm sorry to intrude sir, ma'am. I'm Agent Adam O'Connor with the DEA. I need to ask your daughter a few questions, if I may." Adam hated to interrupt the family bonding, but he needed to find out if this case was in any way related to his partner's disappearance.

"She's not awake. And we don't want her upset. Don't you think she's been through enough?" Mrs. Tate turned back to Sandra's still form. She straightened the cotton blanket with shaking fingers and brushed her daughter's lank dark hair away from her forehead before lifting the girl's limp hand and clasping it to her breast.

"Honey, calm down. You aren't doing you or Sandra any good this way." He squeezed her shoulders before letting go and with a last look at his unconscious child, moved toward the doorway. "Maybe we could talk outside? I don't want to upset my wife anymore."

Adam hesitated, but he couldn't very well shake the girl awake, so he reluctantly followed Mr. Tate out the door and down the corridor to the Sassafras Cafeteria. They each grabbed a cup of coffee and then moved out of the bustle to a quiet table in a corner of the large room. He gave the man time to gather his thoughts before attempting any conversation. He'd never had a child, but could sympathize with the Tate's distress. His own partner, Maggie Holt, had gone undercover months ago in an effort to take down a crime ring known for drugs, money laundering, and human trafficking. Maggie thought they'd caught a break a few months ago when Adam's old SEAL team came under scrutiny, though he'd sworn they were innocent.

A few years earlier the team was involved in an ambush and he'd been shot and reported dead. Instead, the DEA had saved his hide, and demanded payment with his soul. Needless to say, the reunion last spring hadn't gone as smooth as he would've wished. Some of his 'brothers' were hurt by what they saw as his betrayal. Like he'd had a choice. When 'Uncle' says jump, the standard answer is "How high?"

And now Maggie was missing.

Forcing the bitterness aside, Adam focused on the middle-aged man across the plastic cafeteria table from him. Tate looked beaten down, as only a man who'd just learned of how close he'd come to never seeing his daughter again, could look. He mindlessly added packet after packet of sugar to his rapidly cooling coffee as he stared out the window at the dreary day. Thump, thump, rip. Thump, thump, rip.

"You have any children, Agent...was it, Connor?" His voice was low and rumbly, filled with suppressed emotions.

Adam cleared his own throat before replying, "O'Connor, and no I don't, sir." He hated this part of his job. They actually trained for this kind of shit, if you can believe it. How to question the bereaved. Like there could ever be an easy way through this kind of minefield. "I'm sorrier than you could imagine that this had to happen to your family. But, the good news is, you have your girl back."

Tate barked out a harsh sound of disbelief. "Back? You think just because she's up there in that room right now, our lives will go back to normal?" His hand slapped the table; the empty sugar wrappers flew up like discarded confetti. "That's not my little girl. The person in that bed is broken. Our lives are ruined. How do you propose I fix that, Agent O'Connor?"

Adam winced inside. How indeed? "One step at a time, sir. One step at a time."

The angry man before him crumpled and Adam's heart bled for the family. From his reports he'd read Sandra was a smart, well-liked young woman. She'd worked at a local grocery store three nights a week after school. On the night of the abduction she'd left the house as usual, but didn't showed up at her job. The supervisor assumed she was sick and never called the family. Their first inkling something had gone horribly wrong came the next morning when they realized Sandra's bed had not been slept in.

"Look, I know this is hard for you, but if there's anything at all you can tell me..."

Tate looked up with red-rimmed eyes, "What does my daughter's case have to do with the DEA?" His gaze turned suspicious, "Why is some US Secret Service guy here in Canada, wanting to speak with my child?" His voice had risen with each word. Adam glanced around to make sure no one was eavesdropping before turning his gaze back to the distraught parent.

"Your daughter may be involved in an on-going case of human trafficking, Mr. Tate." And as the man's eyes went wide with shock, "this is a wide-spread organization. Your government and mine have teamed up to put an end to these people's activities, but I need your help." Adam waited for his words to sink in. "I'm sure you don't want this to happen to another young girl. Please, sir, let me talk to your daughter," he pleaded.

Tate stared down at his hands squeezing the life out of the Styrofoam coffee cup. Adam held his breath, and waited. Finally, the man stood and growled, "Let's go."

Adam exhaled his relief and hurried to follow Tate before he changed his mind. When they arrived back to the room he noticed there'd been a guard change and had to pull out his ID again in order to enter. Rather than getting annoyed, he was glad the RCMP were taking the danger to his victim seriously. Because if she had escaped a trafficking ring alive, she was a threat to the organization and they would not hesitate to have her killed.

After getting clearance, he entered the room and stumbled to a halt at the touching tableau. Sandra had woken up and the three Tate's were holding each other as if they'd never let go. If he ever got Maggie back, he'd be tempted to do the same. Adam gave them a few moments alone, then coughed to get their attention. The elder couple reluctantly released their daughter and Adam got his first good look at the figure in the bed. Frail. If he had to come up with a term to describe her condition, that would be it. She reminded him of the withered leaves he'd seen on his way to the hospital, tossed here and there by the slightest breeze. Weightless. Her hand had a protruding needle attached to the tube of liquid rehydrating her depleted body.

Adam moved a little farther into the room, but stayed well back from the bed. Even with her parents' right beside her, he could feel the fear radiating from her slight body. He cleared his throat again; suddenly awkward where normally he held control.

"Sandra, I'm Agent O'Connor, Adam." He ignored the parents' start of surprise to concentrate on the girl. "I know this must be difficult for you. I just have a couple of questions." He used all his will power to get her to look him in the eye and see how important this was to him. "My friend, Maggie, is missing. Just like you were." He held out a picture of him and Maggie on his boat a couple of years before. "I was kind of hoping you might have seen her. She has long black hair and light brown eyes..."

Sandra looked at the photograph and jerked. The beep, beep, beep of the heart monitor picked up its rhythm, betraying her anxiety. Her mother immediately hit the buzzer for assistance and Tate moved towards Adam with the obvious intention of making him leave.

"Sandra, please, was Maggie there? Is she okay? Did she get away?" He couldn't control the desperation in his voice as Tate shoved him backward, badge or no badge. Adam knew his time was over. "Sandra?"

He gave her one last pleading look before turning towards the door, and that's when he heard the words he'd been praying for.

"She saved my life."

CHAPTER EIGHTEEN

Jared yawned and stretched—then froze. He wasn't alone. A soft, warm body had trapped one of his arms to the bed. The other hand flexed on a smooth, bare hip. His nose, buried in a fragrant cloud of citrus-scented hair gave him the answer even before his eyes opened on the burnished locks.

Annie.

He'd dreamed of her like this many times over the years. Both before, and after, they'd come together one hot summer's night in a fiery explosion of passion. Jared had a hard time explaining to himself why he'd run the next morning. Because that's exactly what he'd done. At the time, he'd used the excuse of his mom's refusal to support his decision to follow in his father's footsteps by joining the Navy—but that's all it was, an excuse. The real reason he'd run was laying in this bed next to him right now.

Annie Campbell terrified him.

She was everything he'd always wanted, wrapped up in a delectable parcel labeled forever. And that had sent him running for the nearest plane. Because no matter how much he wanted her, he'd thought he wanted the Navy more. After living with what a decision like that had done to his own family, Jared swore never to place someone who loved him through the same torture. He'd had to stand by as a child and watch his mother age before his eyes every time the phone rang. And then, one day, it happened. Only instead of a call, it was the doorbell. Two smartly dressed naval officers stood on the doorstep; hat in hand, solemn looks on their faces, and as his mom broke down with heart-wrenching sobs, Jared knew his father would not be returning.

In the weeks and months that followed, a determination grew within him to find out for himself why his dad chose to risk his life overseas rather than stay home and care for his family. It became an obsession; coloring everything he did, from exercise to bringing his grades up in school. All done with the goal of entering the Navy, not realizing he was becoming the man he'd loved and hated with such passion.

Then he met Annie, and for a while he'd dared to dream. She was shy, withdrawn, a bookworm, whereas he took pleasure in being the class clown. The boy who made everyone laugh. Something about her drew him from the start. He'd often find himself staring at her, fantasizing about those soft, sweet curves. Wondering about the thoughts going on behind those gorgeous green eyes.

One day a couple of guys from his wrestling club accosted her in the hall. When he rounded the corner they were shoving her toward the men's room. A red haze descended. When it cleared the boys were on the floor, dazed and bleeding. They got up calling him crazy, and stumbled off. Embarrassed that he'd lost control, Jared made sure she was okay then disappeared. He should have stayed away, but couldn't. Even then she'd brought out the urge to protect and cherish. At least he'd had the sense to keep their relationship platonic. The last thing in the world he wanted to do was hurt her.

And yet, as he felt her begin to waken in his arms, he knew that's exactly what he had done. Her bare bottom snuggled up against his rapidly growing hard-on and she rubbed her cheek against his forearm with a little mewling sound. He stifled a groan and knew exactly when she regained full consciousness. Her lush body stiffened to a board and her breathing all but stopped, before her heart beneath his hand jumped and then pounded with the force of a gavel.

"Good morning," he whispered against her earlobe, and smiled at her uncontrollable shiver.

She turned onto her back in a startled rush, and then it was him quivering in reaction to her breasts laid out before him like a bountiful feast. Her honey-tinted nipples distended, whether due to the cool air or his rapacious gaze he wasn't sure. But he damn sure appreciated the view he received, except then she covered herself.

"Good morning," she muttered in a wobbly voice. Her cheeks became a mottled pink when her gaze flitted to his face and away. Tense fingers plucked at the end of the sheet as if she wished she could hide. Jared scowled and his brows knitted together. He hadn't expected another declaration of love—okay, maybe he

had—but this threw him for a loop. His arm had
slid from her hip when she turned and now lay
near the danger zone. His fingers tingled with the
desire to touch all that silky skin once more, but
first he needed to find out what was wrong.

He leaned over and placed his lips against her
unresponsive mouth. It took some cajoling before
she finally softened on a sigh of mingled breath.
Her arms crept away from their stranglehold on
the poor sheet, up around his neck into his hair,
and Jared's whole body hummed in response. He
throbbed with the urge to bury himself in her
slick warmth, and had to force himself to hold
back, take his time. His hand moved up to her
cheek and gently smoothed her curly hair back
from her eyes. They opened and Jared thought he
could happily drown in their crystalline depths.
Tears formed and he kissed them away. His
mouth moved back to hers and urged it open, to
let him in. This time when they came together
was different, elemental. A bonding.

The dream held her in a viselike grip. Annie
was powerless to stop the events from happening,
even though she sensed it would be devastating.
She raced through the trees, the low-hanging
skeletal branches yanking at her hair in the
moonless night. Her breathing was loud in the
silence, the urgency to get over the next hill all-
consuming. She fell near the top, scraping her
knees on the rocks, and crawled the rest of the
way, her fingers scrambling for purchase on the
steep slope. The moon teased her with a view of a
cabin by the sparkling water before everything

slid to shadow. Annie started down the other side, compelled by a force larger than herself to get to that cabin as fast as possible. The next flash by the fickle moon made her gasp with relief. Chris and Jessica appeared in the open doorway, the light from inside highlighting their little bodies. She opened her mouth to call out to them, then sucked in a harsh breath of dismay when a tall man in a trench coat shoved them onto the steps, a gun in his hand.

Her dirty, scraped palms rose to block the screams welling up in her throat. *Please, don't hurt them. Please, God, don't let him hurt them.*

The moon dipped behind another cloud and then, like a curtain on a bad vignette, pulled back to reveal Jared standing on the wharf, hands in the air. Jessica sobbed and Chris grabbed her hand, throwing a frightened glance over his shoulder at the dark, menacing figure standing over them. Jared shouted something...she couldn't make it out, and the monster barked out a triumphant laugh.

"I warned you, Martin. I always play to win." His spectral voice floated across the distance.

Jared lowered his arm enough to glance at his watch, then smiled. "So do I, my friend. So do I." And then a series of explosions ripped the skies apart. The children cried out in terror, Annie ducked, her horrified gaze locked on the tableau below. Jared rushed the stairs, but a sudden blast halted his forward momentum. Blood blossomed across the front of his white shirt, and a look of shocked anger crossed his face before he fell sideways into the water with a sickening splash.

A hand touched her shoulder and Annie came up out of the bed fighting, her heart racing and skin clammy with fear. Her fist glanced off a cheekbone and knocked glasses askew before stopped by a warm palm.

"Whoa there, slugger. You could take out an eye that way." Jared's laughing tones woke her from the nightmare. Annie sagged in his arms, breath racing and sweaty, relieved he wasn't feeding the fishes at the bottom of some nameless lake. But then the rest of the dream caught up to her and she began to weep in earnest.

"Honey, don't cry, it's only an eye. I've got another one," Jared teased from above her head as he pulled her up tight to his uninjured chest. His heart beat solidly beneath her ear and his hand gently rubbed up and down her bare back until gradually her waterworks slowed.

Annie tipped her head and stared up into the face of the only man she'd ever loved. His hair damp from a recent shower, smelled fresh and citrusy from her shampoo. Delicious. In another time this would be a fantasy come true. But until they found her child safe and sound, she couldn't think about possibilities. Everything else had to wait.

"How long was I asleep?"

"An hour. And before you ask, no, there hasn't been any calls." He leaned down and kissed her nose. "Why don't you have a quick shower while I make us a coffee, and then we'll go see what your friend, Jack, has come up with, okay?"

She hesitated, knowing they needed to talk about what had just happened between them, and so much more. But, that also, would have to wait.

She nodded and waited for him to exit her bedroom, before dragging herself into the bathroom. Her body, sensitized from their lovemaking, felt both strange and wonderful. She wanted to revel in the moment. If only her son were safe. A glance in the mirror showed her what she already knew, she was a hot mess. Hair going every which way, dark rings under her eyes, puffy lips. Her tongue crept out to grab a last taste of Jared before she hopped into the tub. Mm, something dark and dangerously addictive. Like chocolate.

Annie climbed into the shower and set the water before letting it sluice down over her head, clearing the cobwebs. The first thing on her list was to get back to Jack's office and find out if he'd had any luck tracing the stolen car yet. If they didn't hear something soon, she'd drive every road in the county herself. Her son needed her. The waiting was the hard part. Every minute took him farther away. And if she kept that thought process she be panicking, which wouldn't do anyone any good. Sucking in a wobbly breath, Annie straightened her shoulders. Think constructive, not negative. She could do this. She had to.

The muted rumble of Jared talking to someone had her rush to finish dressing, and hurry down the hall to the kitchen. He stood gazing out the window over the sink, one hand holding a cell to his ear, the other clenched on the edge of the countertop. His stance worried her. She waited for him to speak, not caring that she was eavesdropping.

"Dammit, Chief, I don't know what to do. My hands are tied until that son-of-a-bitch calls with his demands." He shook his head and rubbed the back of his neck, "I hate this waiting, Frank. If the fucker wants to play games, he should play with someone his own size, not a couple of little kids. This is bullshit."

There was silence for a few moments while the person on the other end obviously tried to calm Jared down, because slowly his shoulders eased and she heard a rough sigh. "Okay, sounds good. See you in a few." He set the phone down, then turned to face her, no sign of surprise showing in his grim eyes, before he visibly tried to lighten the mood.

"How'd you know I was here?" she asked, moving toward him now that the call had ended.

"Reflection," he smiled at her bemused look. "There, in the glass, I could see you watching me. Pretty hot, babe."

She ignored his obvious ploy to distract her from the conversation. "Who's Frank? What's good? Can he help us find the kids?" She halted in front of him and he reached out and drew her into his embrace.

"Yes, he can help. Frank is my old CO, and best friend. He's on the way here from Texas and will meet us at the sheriff's office so we can coordinate our efforts."

"And you couldn't have told me this sooner?" Annie leaned away, anxious to get back to the office where she could be in the midst of the rescue effort. Jared's arms tightened their hold, and she glanced up impatiently. "What?"

He just looked at her for a long, quiet moment, willing her to settle down. Slowly the frustration vanished, replaced with an unfamiliar sensation of relief. Relief that she wasn't in this alone, she had Jared's full support. For so many years Annie had handled every crisis, from flus to cuts and scrapes, it felt strange to give up some of the responsibility to someone else. His eyes staring into her own were beautiful, a rich green-blue, reminding her of the Caribbean. Everyone said Chris had her eyes, but she disagreed. He had both his mom and his dad's. They were a family. The thought filled her up like an expanding balloon.

A soft sigh escaped. "I'm sorry. I know you're doing everything you can." She met his gaze, "Thank you for calling your friend."

He leaned down and planted a soft kiss against her mouth, "You're welcome."

Annie and Jared arrived back at sheriff headquarters to an onslaught of phones ringing, answered by harried officers and volunteers rushing in and out, many stopping to hug and reassure her. Jack stood tall and commanding in the midst of the chaos. The moment he noticed her he started forward, a warm light entering his eyes. Then he spotted Jared, his arm wrapped proprietarily around her waist, and halted. The glow faded, replaced by resignation. Jack nodded toward his office, then turned away to speak to a nearby officer Annie recognized as being the husband of one of her regular customers.

As soon as the door closed behind them, Annie broke away from Jared's touch and strode across to the desk. She hated herself for hurting Jack. He was a good man. A man who deserved someone's love and devotion. She felt bad for letting him down, but the silent man grimly regarding her from his spot by the window had stole her heart many years ago. The light played with the textures of his hair, turning it to molten gold. He'd crossed his strong arms and the rolled up sleeves of his faded denim shirt displayed his colorful tats as well as his latent strength. Power she'd felt not very long ago when he'd swept her into his arms and carried her away, like a buccaneer with his conquest.

Her face warmed, and she looked around for something to take her mind off how Jared had ravished her. An open file by Jack's half-empty coffee cup caught her attention. Actually the name, Jared Martin, scrawled in black ink across the top of the page drew her eye first. She glanced up, but Jared had turned away and seemed lost in thought as he stared out onto the tree-lined street, so she sat in Jack's chair and began to read. It contained a complete dossier. From his birth in Tidal Falls General Hospital at eight pounds, six ounces, to his antics at school. Then as a teen when his father died overseas and the carefree boy changed overnight. She read how his grades began to climb—this was about the time they'd met—and his interest in sports grew. She smiled at a notation from his physics teacher on his natural ability with electrical instrumentation. He'd always tinkered with radios and computers when they got together at his house for studying. The memory was bittersweet.

Jack's deep voice from the other side of the door startled her. She looked up guiltily, but then it faded away. Jared hadn't moved, and she briefly wondered what he was thinking about, but then the pages she'd not yet read pulled her attention.

She skimmed down to where he'd left home, traveled to Coronado where he enlisted in the Navy. Straight from there he took his test and was accepted into SEAL training. Annie's brow furrowed as she read of something called Hell Week where he had to train continuously for five days and five nights with a maximum of four hours sleep. Why would anyone in their right minds put themselves through that? She gazed at his proud bearing and thought she knew—his father. Jared idolized the man, even as he hated him for leaving them. He'd shared little of those days with her, but Annie sensed his thoughts of his father were often turbulent. Pushing and pulling, much like the drag of the sea he'd trained in.

She turned to the next page and read how he'd graduated with honors to become a member of SEAL team five under the command of Senior Chief Frank Stein. Ah, so this is Jared's friend, Frank. Now she was beginning to understand Jared's confidence that his CO could help them where the local PD might not. The more she read, the more she grasped that he had belonged to an elite fighting force. Warriors. If anyone could find her son and bring him home, these men would.

There wasn't much about the team's deployments, only the casualties they'd brought back. And there were many. From knife wounds, to mortar shots, to loss of limb from improvised explosive devices—IED's. While she'd been home raising a child on her own, Jared was fighting for his country—and to stay alive. It humbled her. As she followed the trail of his life for the past eight years, her pride for him grew, even when she read of his gambling and subsequent arrest for mischief a few months ago. She'd heard of soldiers returning from war with varying degrees of P.T.S.D. The symptoms ranged anywhere from nightmares and flashbacks, to detachment and self-destructive behavior. This went a long way to explaining Jared's avoidance of home and family over the years. He'd cut himself off from those who loved him the most.

"What are you reading?" Jared's voice coming from over her shoulder startled her. She hurried to close the file, flipping it over. No need for him to know Jack had him investigated.

Annie pushed the chair back and stood, effectively blocking his view of the desk. "Nothing, just wasting time. What do you think is taking so long?"

Jared looked skeptical, but let the matter drop. "I don't know. It's a madhouse out there though. It's good to see the town still stands behind its citizens in times of crisis."

Her throat tightened. Sudden tears blurred her vision. Jared cursed, realizing what he'd said, "Shit, Annie, I didn't mean it that way. C'me 'ere, love." He held out his arms and she walked into their enveloping warmth. His hand cradled her head against his chest. She inhaled the mixed scents of pine and citrus.

"I'm just so scared, Jared. I'm barely holding it together. What's taking so long? Why can't they find them?" Her voice wavered and hands clenched his shirt as frustration overwhelmed her.

"I know, baby, I kno..." the door opened, cutting off whatever he'd been about to say. Jack stomped in looking ready to hurt someone, followed by a dark giant who dwarfed the doorway. Jared released his grip on her back, but grasped her hand drawing her with him as he made a beeline for the stranger.

"You made it, about damn time. What took you so long?" The words belied by a shit-eating grin, Jared released her hand to smack the stranger's bulldog shoulder.

Annie cringed.

The hulk gave him a lopsided smile and a lightning fast return jab that set Jared back a couple of paces. "Next time maybe I won't come at all."

Jared rubbed his arm, where there would surely be a bruise, and grinned back, "Yeah, you will. You know you love me."

"I'd love to choke you, you mean. What did you get yourself into this time?" he asked, nodding toward Jack.

"It wasn't me, Chief, I swear. Nick asked me to take care of Jake while he and Sara took a trip and next thing you know that guy I had the run-in with at the casino turns up here, of all places." Jared cursed and ran a hand through his hair in agitation before spinning away to pace across the room and back.

"Somehow he found out about my friendship with Annie. He went to her store and scared her with a warning directed at me."

"Hi, I'm Annie, and you must be Frank." Annie held her hand out, tired of being talked over. Frank hesitated, then held out his own beefy mitt for a quick shake. His eyes, a quicksilver grey, took a moment to take her measure, then he gave a slight nod, as if in approval. That was good, because Annie didn't think she wanted to be on this man's bad side. "I really appreciate you traveling all this way to help me out." She sent a reproachful look Jared's way, but he just shrugged.

"It's no problem, miss. Jared and I go way back, there's not much I wouldn't do for him."

"Ditto, my brother-from-another-mother. Sorry, man, I do appreciate you coming, you know that." Jared shifted his feet and glanced at Jack, who'd trolled over to his desk and fired up the computer. "We have a bad situation here, Frank. That jackass grabbed two kids last night, Sara's daughter, Jessica, plus Annie and..." He stumbled to a halt. Then his gaze locked on her, he finished, "and my son. He has them both."

An awkward silence filled the room. Annie couldn't look at Jack. She wasn't ashamed of her relationship with Jared, but wished she could have told him privately. It had to have been a shock. Jared's face remained solemn as he tried to gage how she felt with his confession.

Confused. Shaken. Elated.

She'd just stretched her hands out to his when Jack's gruff voice reached across the room with the force of a sledgehammer.

"He's made contact."

CHAPTER NINETEEN

Sergei shut down the throwaway he'd purchased at a gas station in Seattle. The last thing he needed was a trace on his messages. He imagined the frustrated anger on Martin's face when he read the e-mail sent to the sheriff's office in that little shithole town of his. A whistled sigh of satisfaction slid past his lips. He glanced at the children asleep on the bed. Unlike Chenglei, he meant them no harm. They would be safe enough with him. Unless Martin didn't fulfill his demands, then all bets were off. He tossed another log into the potbelly stove and lifted his hands to the warmth.

Driving country roads for what seemed like hours in the dark, the deserted cabin had suddenly risen out of the landscape as if calling to him. The overgrown drive and porch full of fallen leaves told him it was probably a summer getaway. He'd locked the kids in the trunk, ignoring the pleading sobs. Then, gun in hand, he checked the area, freezing when the stairs creaked beneath his weight. When nothing moved within, he did a quick search by the light on his phone. The window was layered with musty smelling dust and showed a single room, bed in the corner, wooden table and chairs, and the stove. He'd found the key under the flowerpot, and opened the creaky door. On a small countertop with a single sink, he found a kerosene lantern and matches. His nose crinkled with the pungent aroma as he pumped the lamp, then lit the wick.

To ward off the chilly fall night, he'd started a small fire in the stove. They were far enough away he felt reasonably safe, at least until daybreak when the search would move to high gear. Next he went back to the kids. Guilt grabbed hold when he opened the lid on their terrified faces. To combat it, he said, "Unless you want to stay here in the dark, do as I say."

Two little heads, one blond the other red, bobbed in agreement. The girl stared at him with Betty Boop eyes, while the boy glared. Just like Martin.

"What are you g...going to do with us?" the girl stuttered.

"Nothing—if you listen." Sergei warned. He noticed them shivering and scowled. "Get yourselves out of there and into the house. And no funny stuff." Strangely loathe to pull the gun on them, he placed a hand in his pocket and stuck a finger out, hinting. He almost laughed at how fast they scurried out of the trunk and up those stairs.

He'd found a folded quilt in the narrow closet, threw it on the bed, and told them to sleep. While they settled down Sergei made a pot of coffee from grounds located in the pantry, and soon the old shack seemed almost homey. Not for long though, Martin would be on his trail, sniffing him out like a Bloodhound.

Sergei had done his homework in the past months and knew what he was up against. A Navy fricken SEAL. What had begun as a revenge tactic was quickly growing out of control. The original plan had entailed a little mayhem and maybe some vengeance to prove his worth with his superiors. Sergei wished he'd taken more time to find Martin on his own, rather than involving the cartel. Instead he owed Chenglei a debt of honor. One he had no desire to fulfill.

Again his gaze focused on the tiny bodies occupying the double bed, pale faces peeking from beneath the handmade quilt. Had he ever been that innocent? Not that he could remember. The only child of a prostitute in Moscow, Sergei knew it was only a matter of time before he too would be in the tochka forced to submit to the perversion of men and their filthy minds. Desperate not to follow his mother's path he joined one of the many gangs roaming the streets. They took him in on the condition he earned his keep— as a pickpocket. He'd been six.

Later Sergei discovered the mafia ran the new 'familia' he'd made. They taught him survival skills, how to fight, and how to kill. When he became a grown man he earned their respect as an enforcer, maintaining control over those he'd feared as a child. The leaders rewarded his loyalty, sending him to America as head of security for their newest enterprise, a casino. And he'd thrived. The Brigadier left him in control, and for the first time in his misbegotten life, Sergei felt worthy. Then Martin had to come along and make a fool of him.

Unforgiveable.

The question now was how to appease Chenglei, who would be expecting compensation for his trouble. He'd thought to pass over the children, thereby killing two birds with one stone, but now found he could not. No matter that at least one of the runts were the offspring of his enemy, his stomach still revolted at the thought of their abuse.

"I gotta pee." The plaintive words startled him from his contemplation of the stove. The boy sat up in bed, his body quaking but defiant just the same. Sergei's throat tightened, the kid reminded him so much of himself. Small but mighty. If he wasn't careful he'd be offering to play games to keep them occupied next. He shook his head, bemused. The boy thought that meant no, and flung himself back, narrowly missing the sleeping girl.

"You going, or do you plan to wet the bed?" Sergei asked, keeping his voice low. The child sat up uncertainly and he waved him to the door in the corner of the room. "Well, hurry it up, then."

The kid skittered out of the bed and ran for the dark bathroom. Eyes watchful, he stood on his toes to reach the wall switch, then carefully shut the door. Sergei grinned. Another minute and the boy might not have made it. The smile went sideways when the girl, sensing she was alone, started to squirm. He held his breath until she settled back down.

What's taking that kid so long?

Shit, he hadn't checked the bathroom for a window. He jumped up, glowering when the wooden chair fell over and woke the girl, who started to sob, "Chris, Chr...ris."

Sergei was almost to the door when it opened and the boy, Chris, hurried through, only to slide to a guilty stop.

"What were you doing in there, boy?" Sergei shoved him aside to glance in the room. No window. He turned to see Chris crawl up the bed and tuck himself close to the frightened girl.

"Don't cry, Jess. I wouldn't leave you here with *him*." He patted her arm awkwardly and shot a glare of hatred toward Sergei's chest.

Okay, good. It was better if they remained scared of him. "Go to sleep," he growled.

Silence reigned for a few blessed minutes. Then he heard a little voice squeak, "I'm hungry."

The clang of the lock against the bars of her jail made Maggie lifted her head from her inspection of Olga's beaten face. Her stomach dropped when Chenglei entered, closely followed by one of his burly guards. The urge to fold herself into a fetal position overwhelmed her, but she refused to give him the satisfaction. Maggie sat up straight on the cold cement floor and pretended instead of naked and dirty she was dressed for a cocktail date. The bastard wore a white suit and carried a cane like he was a southern gentleman out for a fricken stroll. She smoothed Olga's hair behind her ear with gentle fingers, then turned, careful not to let the men see her favoring her side. They were predators. Any sign of weakness would be noted.

"What do you want? People will be looking for us. The police will be searching." Maggie probed his slitted eyes, and hoped her words would gain them some time. "Let us go. We won't say a word, will we?" She nudged Olga's knee and received a grunt in response. Worry over her condition forced the word from Maggie's throat, "Please."

Chenglei's fat head fell back and he shouted with laughter. He drew a blue linen napkin from the breast pocket of his suit and dabbed his eyes, then meticulously folded the cloth and returned it to his jacket.

"I'm going to miss our association—Agent Holt."

Shit. He'd found out she was a fed. Maggie changed gears. Now it was all about survival.

"You do anything to either one of us and even the devil himself won't be able to protect you. My partner and the rest of the team know exactly where I am. If I don't report in as usual, they're going to tear this place apart." She lifted her chin and stared him in the eye. "Do you really want that?"

He eyed her contemptuously for a long moment, and then roamed around their eight-by-eight pen, careful to stay away from the bucket they were privileged to use for necessities.

"You surprise me, Agent Holt. I expected begging and crying; instead you give me attitude and sarcasm. Do you not fear for your life—or that of your friend?"

Maggie wished he'd quit moving around. It made her nervous. "Of course I do, I'd be an idiot if I didn't. But I could ask you the same question. My team isn't known for their patience, Chenglei. You've already kept me in this *pit* for what, a week?" She waited for his answer and when none was forthcoming, "They'll come after you with everything they have. You must realize that. Is it worth your empire to seek revenge on one lone female who managed to trick you?" She knew as soon as she said it, she'd gone too far.

He swung around. The force of his anger tightened his jaw and clenched his fists. He swooped across the enclosure, the cane over his head like the Sword of Damocles.

"Yes," he snarled, spittle foaming from the edges of his lips, and brought the staff swinging downward, his eyes aglow a devil's red with the light of vengeance.

CHAPTER TWENTY

Frank and Jared crowded around the computer screen the moment Jack informed them of a message from the kidnapper. The silence in the room threatened to make Annie scream. *What's going on? What does he want? Where's my son?* She wanted to yank her hair out in frustration. Or maybe Sergei's. *Yeah, definitely his.*

She moved around the desk to find out for herself what the e-mail said, only to get outmaneuvered by the testosterone twins. Now the three oh-so-different heads stood close together pouring over the data coming in from Jack's trace on the text message. From what she could read, the suspect—who would've thought she'd ever use that term—used a throwaway cell phone which made the job of tracing harder, if not impossible. A reverse search of the number seemed to show that he was still in the vicinity, although it couldn't pinpoint location.

Jack initiated an examination of previous call records from that number, his forefinger all but murdering the keyboard. But he warned her they needed to wait for a judge to clear the order. Meanwhile, Frank and Jared had laid a map out on the desk and were triangulating an area going by the ping off nearby cell towers, while she...watched.

Anger and frustration welled up her throat. Her stomach churned with fear. Horrifying pictures of what that creep might be doing to her child, and Sara's daughter, kept playing a repulsive film in her head. She shoved her chair back and headed for the door, suddenly desperate for some fresh air.

"Where are you going?" Jared's worried tone slowed her momentum. She plastered a smile on her face and turned to reassure him.

"I'm just going to grab us a coffee, looks like we'll need it. I'll be right back." Before he could say anything more, she opened the door and slipped through, closing it carefully when slamming it might have helped defuse a bit of the tension. Jack's office had an open floor plan; the room she'd just left opening out into the main bullpen, rather aptly named she thought. There were six desks throughout the area, three of them manned by officers either writing in thick files or scanning computer screens. A secretary, Grace's friend Angie Sorensen, stood at the front counter fielding calls and directing inquiries from the throng near the door.

The moment the crowd noticed Annie, the noise swelled to deafening proportions. "Have they caught him yet?"

"We're so sorry, honey."

"What can we do?"

"Why were the children alone?"

That one hurt. She should have known better, especially after the events of the morning. It was an error in judgment she'd have to live with the rest of her life. Annie just prayed the kids wouldn't be the ones to pay the price.

These people were her friends. They wanted to help, but she couldn't deal with their questions right now so she gave Angie a slight nod indicating the back door. Angie smiled her understanding and turned back to the crowd. "Okay people, listen up. This is how we're going to do this. Anyone with something helpful to say, line up here. Everyone else, out."

Amid disgruntled grumbling and shuffling bodies, Annie snuck out the side door into the relative peace of the parking lot. A picnic table under a weeping willow looked inviting, a good place to regain some perspective. She'd always been a doer and this waiting for the other shoe to drop drove her crazy. It made sense to stay nearby, Jack would get results faster than she could. But, oh how she wanted to be out there searching. If only she knew which way to go.

The warmth of the sun's rays drew her gaze. A stream of light shone down through the leafless branches of the tree reminding her of...that's it, the skeletal branches of her nightmare. Could that frightening dream she'd had this morning actually been a clue? Crazy, but her heart started to pound a message of go, go, go, and her breathing accelerated as if she were back there, on that hill. She'd already risen and started for home and her car when a familiar truck pulled into the lot. Nick and Sara.

Tears pooled and ran down Annie's face as the stricken, pale gaze of her best friend found her through the glare of the windshield. She hurried toward the moving vehicle, ignoring Jared's shouted warning from behind. The squeal of brakes accompanied by a flood of swearing stopped her in her tracks. She glanced around dazed.

Jared jogged to her side, his face a grim mask. He grabbed her arm and swung her around. "Annie, Christ, do you want to get killed?" His voice shook with anger and fear as he hauled her into his arms.

She opened her mouth, wanting to apologize, but with a last blazing glance he turned away to meet Nick who'd hopped down from the cab of the truck. Lost, now that she realized how foolish she'd been, Annie turned away from Jared's tense back to greet Sara after Nick helped her down.

"Are you okay? God, Annie, you scared me." Sara rushed to hug her, and as she held on and felt her friend's support and lack of blame, Annie finally broke down.

Jared greeted Nick with a firm handshake and then pulled him in for a man hug. His friend explained how the RCMP came knocking on their cabin door in Port Alice during the middle of the night. They'd tried to find a flight back from Nanaimo but were too late, so they'd driven the five hours to Victoria and caught the first ferry available. Through it all, Jared kept an eye on Annie falling apart in Sara's arms. And wished he were the one holding her close. Sara's moist gaze met his over Annie's head and that was it, he was on the move. He nodded reassurance to Sara and turned the sobbing woman who held his heart into his chest, his hold protective.

"Shh, baby, I've got you. It's going to be okay. Shh." Her agony became his pain. He ached with the need to make amends and bring their son home.

Nick moved behind Sara and wrapped his arms around her waist. She looked up and gave him a brief kiss, before turning back to Jared, her gaze looking for answers he didn't have.

His throat tightened with regret. "I'm sorry, Sara. I don't know what else to say. I'd never knowingly bring danger to those kids. I can't believe this even fricken happened."

She reached over and ran a gentle hand over Annie's crazy curls, and Jared was relieved when her sobs eased up, and her body relaxed in his hold. Give him a room full of insurgents any day over a crying woman. Especially this crying woman.

"There's nothing for you to be sorry for, Jared. From what Nick told me after he got through to Sheriff Garrett, you did everything you could." Sara leaned against her fiancé's chest, her arms wrapping his in a layer of love. "Let's leave the blame to the bad guys and get our children home."

Jared and Nick looked at each other, and a slow smile lit their eyes. *Hooyah.* Then Jared leaned down and gently kissed the tears from Annie's face. "C'mon, honey, let's go in and see how Frank and the sheriff are coming along."

She raised her head, her nose red and eyes swollen. "Can I talk to you for a minute, privately?"

Nick coughed and glanced around. "Frank's here? Why didn't you say so? Let's go find the big guy and say hi, Sara." His obvious ploy to give them a moment brought a slight twist of a smile from Annie.

"Don't worry, we'll be right behind you," she said, then the two women hugged again, one tall, slim and blond, the other a little shorter, curvy with russet waves that twisted around his heart. Annie stared broodingly after her friend until they disappeared from view, then she turned to him, a look of determination lighting her features. "I think I might know where they are."

Jared's mouth fell open in surprise. "What do you mean, you know where they are? How?"

Annie looked away, as if embarrassed, then lifted her chin and blurted it out. "I had a dream."

He rocked back on his heels and crossed his arms, waiting for the punch line.

"I'm serious. This morning. Remember, I hit you?"

He slowly nodded. Where was she going with this?

"Well...there was a cabin, by a lake, and the kids were there." Annie's voice dropped to a murmur, "With your friend, Sergei."

Jared dropped his arms, and reached out to lift her chin so he could see what she was thinking. "First, he's not my friend. And second," He pulled her toward him and gave in to the temptation to peck at those kissable lips until she softened for him. A groan escaped. His arms tightened, tipping her back and up to meet mouth to mouth, his body hardening in a passion-fueled rush. His hands moved down to her plump ass and squeezed, lifting her against him. When her tongue flicked out delicately to taste him, Jared swore. If they weren't in such a public place he'd have her down on the ground under that willow tree right now. There'd be no stopping. He felt like a horny teenager again.

Reluctant, he slowed their momentum, and with a last lingering kiss, lifted his head to gaze into her flushed face. Her eyes slid open and were a green to rival the deepest mountain meadow. He could lie in their depths for an eternity and it still wouldn't be long enough.

"Marry me."

Hard to say which one of them was more shocked. Annie's eyes grew wide and her still glistening mouth dropped open. His heart refused to beat, his hands grew clammy, and his forehead broke out in a sweat. The breeze quit blowing and the birds went silent. It seemed as if the whole world hushed.

"Yes."

One small word and yet it carried the power to bring him to his knees. *Holy shit.* Jared stared into her smiling, crying face highlighted by an impossibly blue sky, and his whole world narrowed down to this moment. Unexpected tears welled up, blurring his vision, and he blinked rapidly, trying to keep her in focus. Her hands held within his, shook so hard he could barely hold on. She sank to meet him face to face and wiped the moisture from his cheeks with trembling fingers before swiping at her own eyes.

"Yes?" he whispered, not believing his ears. Not sure where the words had come from, only that it felt right. More than right.

Her smile peeked out and warmed the air between them with its glow. "Yes, yes, a thousand times yes." She wrapped slim arms around his neck and held on with a death grip, her nose buried into his collar, and Jared's eyes slid closed in a silent thanks to the powers that be. They still needed to find their child, but now with her by his side, he felt like Superman. Indestructible.

Inside the sheriff's office, Jack turned away from the window. He felt like a voyeur on the tableau taking place in his parking lot. Annie seemed happy with the guy, and if Jared's reaction were anything to go by, they'd be a good match. Jack couldn't deny he was disappointed, but he wasn't heartbroken, thank Christ. Oh, he'd miss their dates, they'd had a lot of fun together, something in short supply these days. But he'd been down that road once, had the daughter to prove it, and had no intention of ever going there again. Love hurts. Speaking of which, when this mess got straightened out, he planned on spending some quality time with Tina. This case brought home how easy it is to take for granted those most important to you, until it was too late.

As he observed them reuniting across the room Jack admitted to envy. Martin had a strong network of friends. His own family, three sisters and his brother, Ty, all lived within a couple hundred miles of Tidal Falls, yet they were nowhere near this close. They got together at holidays and once in a while Ty hosted a shindig over at his place, wherein they all arrived, ate, and left in the space of two hours. Pathetic really, when you considered they were blood relatives.

A radiant Annie and strutting Jared reentered the room and everyone gathered around like proud parents. Excited, Annie broke the news of the upcoming nuptials and there was a round of backslapping and hugging. Amid the laughter and chatter their eyes met, and with a hesitant smile, she made her way over.

"Did you hear?" She examined his face, her eyes losing some of their sparkle. He didn't want that, she deserved happiness, and if that meant Martin, so be it.

"I did." Then, realizing how perilously close that was to a marriage vow, he added, "I'm happy for you, Annie.

"I'm sorry, Jack. I never meant to hurt you."

She looked so soulful he had to let her off the hook. "I'm okay, darlin'. A little bruised, but not battered. As long as you're happy, I'm good."

"You'll meet the right woman some day, Jack Garrett, and she'll knock those size eleven feet right out from under you, mark my words." She cast a glance over her shoulder as Jared joined them, and the glow returned.

"It's size nine, miss, and I won't hold my breath." He turned to the others, "Nick, Sara, good to have you back, sorry it's for this reason." They nodded, both of their faces travel-worn and worried. "I'm not sure how much you were told so far, so I think a recap now that we're all here is a good idea."

He went over the details, starting with Annie's break-in, and subsequent kidnapping of the children, Christopher Campbell, age seven, and Jessica Reid, age eight. Both sets of parents held their loved ones hands clenched tight for strength. Jack hoped they wouldn't need it.

Frank Stein had stayed back, quiet throughout the preliminaries, but now he cleared his throat. "Have you received a report on Barnikov yet?"

Yeah, as a matter of fact he had, and it wasn't good. He shuffled the files on his desk, not missing the fact that someone had gone through Garrett's papers.

"Sergei Barnikov, born 1975 Moscow, Russia. Father unknown, mother sex-trade worker. Near as we can tell, he joined a local street gang at age six or seven and started out as a pickpocket. From there Barnikov graduated to armed robbery and kidnapping for the mafia." Jack looked up from the open file. "This guy's a career criminal. Rewarded for his dedication, Sergei was given the esteemed position of head of security for the Golden Nugget casino in Las Vegas, Nevada— where I believe you two first met?" He met Jared's eye and received a frown in reply.

"At least we now know his motive, vengeance. You made a fool of him before his superiors." Jared opened his mouth, and Jack cut him off. "I'm not saying he didn't deserve what you did, and a whole lot more. I saw the LVPD pictures. It's just that maybe now we understand his reasoning, we can prepare for his next move."

"Which will be what? I'm the one he wants. Why doesn't the fu...nut come after me?" Jared slammed his hand on the edge of the desk before turning away in disgust.

"Jared." Annie followed, her hand going to his tense back. "That's not the answer. We need to think with our heads, not our emotions. Believe me, I want Chris and Jessica back more than anything, but if we leap into this, it could get them hurt."

Frank's deep voice broke the strained moment, "He knows that, miss. We've trained countless hours for missions just like this, the capture of hostages. Jared knows his job; he's one of the best. He's just blowing off a little steam, is all."

Nick hugged Sara close and agreed. "Chief's right, we'll get them back. Where's Jake? We might need his nose."

"Probably asleep on my bed. Who taught him to be a pillow hog?" Jared griped, but a smile lit his eyes and his posture relaxed. He reached over his shoulder and brought Annie's palm to his lips.

Just then the phone rang and a new tension filled the room. Jack hesitated for a brief second before catching it on the second ring, "Sheriff's office." He pulled a battered notepad out of the drawer and listened to the man on the other end. The more he heard, the worse it got. Knowing the others needed to hear this he halted his caller mid-sentence. "Hold up there, I have some friends of yours here. They better have a listen, I'm turning on the speaker."

Feeling the brunt of five pairs of eyes trained on him, Jack faced the room. "I have DEA Special Agent Adam O'Connor on the line. I remember he's an acquaintance from when he was here last spring to capture your ex-husband, Sara. Is this correct?" The men slowly nodded; likely they knew this wasn't a reunion call. "He has information pertaining to our case. I'll put him through now."

There was a click, and a brief moment of silence, then Agent O'Connor's voice rang out as clear as if he were standing before them. "Who's there? Damn it, Sheriff, this is a classified matter, you can't go sharing it with the whole town."

"Take it easy, you blowhard. It's us." Nick grinned at the phone.

Another second of silence, then, "Nick? Is that you? I thought you were off on an orgy convention."

Nick burst out laughing and Sara turned a brilliant red. "Careful, buddy, my beautiful fiancé can whip your skinny ass."

"Whoops, sorry Sara. That's why I like video conferencing. Who else is there?"

"The whole gang, Frank, Jared, Sara's friend Annie—not sure if you met her, and Sheriff Garrett. What's going on?"

"Well, that's what I was hoping the sheriff could tell me. I understand his department put out an APB on one Sergei Barnikov. This Barnikov has direct ties to organized crime, and specifically to a case I'm working involved with human trafficking." He stopped to let that sink in and Jack stared grimly at the new horror developing on the women's faces. Christ, he knew this wasn't going to be good.

Jack cleared his throat and then did his job, laying out the facts they'd just gone over to Agent O'Connor. "Now what does Barnikov have to do with your case?" It was a question they needed to know, but were scared to get the answer.

"Sara, Annie, I'm so sorry. I'm on my way there right now, we'll catch him, I promise." The people in the room looked at each other.

"Why does the DEA need to involve themselves in a local kidnapping case?" And please God don't say these were child molesters. Jack held his breath, as he was sure everyone else did.

"Because Barnikov is in bed with a Mexican cartel leader who goes by the name, Chenglei. He made a deal to launder the cartel's dirty money through his casino in return for a favor. To find one slippery Navy SEAL, Jared Martin."

"If you knew he was coming after me, and I'd like to know how, then why the hell didn't you warn me?" Jared said, his posture saying it was a good thing O'Connor wasn't in the room right now. "We could have avoided this whole thing and those kids would be home, safe, you asshole."

"Jared," Frank and Nick warned at the same time.

"Don't Jared me. First the fucker disappears for five fricken years, then he shows up and it's been nothing but Goddamn chaos ever since."

"Jared, calm down, this won't help bring the children home. Kill each other if you want later, for now, let's focus." Annie's shaky voice over his shoulder stomped on Jared's rant. He turned, and with a helpless shrug wrapped his arms around her.

Jack refocused on the caller. Martin was right about one thing, why hadn't the DEA warned them? "You care to spill the rest of the story now you've given us the teaser?"

O'Connor sighed. "My partner, Agent Holt..." Jack noted Frank's sudden rapt attention. "went undercover into Chenglei's organization months ago. She overheard the conversation between Barnikov and our guy and called it in. We kept an eye on the situation but then everything went sideways a month ago and I've been out of contact since."

Frank pushed away from his position on the wall. "What do you mean, out of contact? Don't you have a plan B?"

"Hey, Chief. Yeah we have a B, C, and fricken D. We still can't locate her. Maggie's good, she knows her job, but I don't like it. Something's wrong." Adam's voice wavered in and out like he was going through a tunnel, "...she is. I'll fill you in on the rest when I get there. I'm only a couple hours away."

Frank scowled and turned away, frustration in every line of his linebacker body. Jack reached over and clicked off the now dead phone line. "Well, what's next?"

Annie moved from within Jared's embrace. "I tell you about my dream."

CHAPTER TWENTY-ONE

Annie sat down across from the sheriff's desk, finished her story about the dream she'd had that morning and waited for the fall-out. Mouth dry, her stomach sank. It sounded silly now. As if some vision could lead her to her child. Jack's gaze remained focused on his computer screen, but that click, click of his pen gave away his doubts. Nick and Sara both looked at her with compassion. Sara reached across the space between their chairs to give her a swift floral-scented hug. She couldn't tell what Jared thought, he stood behind her, his comforting hands gently massaging her shoulders.

Frank surprised her by striding from his spot holding up the wall across the room, to crouch by her chair. "That's good, honey, real good." He shot an indecipherable glance up at Jared who gave her arms a squeeze. Then those downy gray eyes—strangely hypnotic in his weathered face—met hers, encouragement glowing within their silvery depths.

"So you don't think I'm an idiot?" Annie shook her head doubtfully.

"Sometimes the subconscious uses our sixth sense to share information it considers important.

It's our job to pay attention. Unfortunately, not enough do, at their own peril." Again, with the meaningful look over her shoulder. "Is there anything else you can recall? Any noticeable landmarks maybe?"

Annie twisted toward her new fiancé. His solid presence warmed her back and gave her the confidence to finish the tale. "That's the funny part, I think I remember where the cabin might be." She turned to Jack. "Didn't the Fowler family own a cottage by Long Lake? Katy used to talk about their family spending summers there every year when we were in school."

Jack nodded, his gaze sharpening. "Ty used to hang with her twin brother, Kyle. I think he went out there with them a couple times."

"Yeah, I remember that too, great fishing as I recall." Jared's voice rumbled from above her head.

Frank smiled into her eyes and it changed his face. The nondescript suddenly became exceptional. Annie blinked. He patted her knee, stood, and moved to the map still laid out on the desk. "Where's that lake?"

Jack pointed. Everyone circled to get a better look. According to the coordinates they'd received from the cell towers, the lake fell squarely in the center of the marked quadrant. Jackpot. Annie had an odd sense of déjà vu as she gazed at the spot Jack circled on the map. Her nerves skittered with the overpowering urgency to rush for the door. Chris was there, she knew it.

"So, let's go." She pushed away from the desk. Her heart filled with anticipation even though her head shouted warnings of the threat they still had to overcome. Jared reached out and caught her hand, stilling her momentum. Annie turned back with an impatient frown. Her eyes met his empathetic gaze. "What? We have to hurry before he moves them." She looked across the table at Sara and Nick who hadn't moved. "You believe me, don't you?"

Sympathy and hope fought for control in Sara's golden eyes. "Of course I do." She leaned over and gave Nick a lingering kiss. His expression filled with so much unabashed love for the woman at his side, the other men coughed uncomfortably. "We all do. But as I learned last year, it doesn't pay to leap before you do a little planning."

Annie sighed, but acknowledged the truth of her friend's words. Sara's abusive ex-husband had caused a lot of heartache and stress when he'd refused to leave her alone. She'd escaped across country to Tidal Falls in a desperate bid for freedom. But he'd tracked her down and held Grace, Sara, and her next-door neighbor, Tess, at gunpoint until the men in this room, and a couple DEA agents managed to get them free.

"Okay fine, so what's the plan then?"

Jared barked out a short laugh. "Were you always this bossy?" He towed her in and hugged her close, placing a warm kiss on her brow. "We'll go, I promise." He looked over her head at Frank and Jack, "How about we head out now and have a look around? You guys can solidify the details and give us a call when you leave."

Frank was shaking his head, "I don't think that's a good idea. You have too much at stake to be objective."

"True that, Chief. But I also know what one wrong step can cost." They stared hard at each other for a long moment, some silent conversation going on that the rest of the party wasn't privy to. "C'mon man. I promise to wait for backup if we get lucky and the prick is holed up out there."

Jack cleared his throat and interjected, "While I appreciate the extra set of hands, let's not forget this is my jurisdiction." He waved a hand at the map. "I happen to agree with Martin. Someone should get out there and check the lay of the land; it may as well be him."

Annie started for the door. Jack swore. "Annie, stop. I said Martin can go, not you."

She swung around in disbelief. Her brows lowered in anger. Her hands crunched together and she wished they were around his neck. "Why, Jack? He's my son, I need to be there."

He met her stormy gaze with a stubborn one of his own. "I'm sorry, but as a civilian I can't let you go racing willy-nilly onto a possible crime scene."

Her legs almost crumpled at his words. Up to this moment Annie hadn't allowed herself to consider what they might find when they located the children. A distant part of her mind acknowledged the shocked cry Sara gave, turning into Nick's chest for comfort. And the disgusted glance Jared sent Jack's way before hurrying to her side. The almost comical dismay on Jack's face, and the stoic look on Frank's. Jared tried to cuddle her close, but she suddenly desperately needed space and jerked away, hating the hurt on his face.

"I...I'm going to the washroom." Her gaze dared anyone to follow before she spun and made her way to the door.

Furious at Jack's thoughtless words, Jared whirled and flew across the room before anyone could make a move to stop him. His fist plowed into the sheriff's jaw and sent him reeling backward into his chair. He started forward with the full intent of knocking the son-of-a-bitch into next week, but rough hands slowed his momentum.

"You stupid asshole. Don't you think she has enough to worry about without throwing it in her face?" Disgusted, he shrugged Frank and Nick off. "I thought you cared about her."

Jack slowly hoisted himself up, and a hand rubbed at the red stain spreading across his cheek. "I do care about her. Do you really want her first on scene if shit hits the fan?" He shook his head. "I wouldn't wish that on my worst enemy, never mind someone I..." he hesitated, then smiled grimly, "know."

Jared's hand clenched, asshole.

"If you two idiots are done with your pissing contest do you think maybe we can focus on finding our children?" Sara stood, hands on hips, glaring at them like they were errant kids.

She was right, this wasn't getting them anywhere. "I'm outta here. Can you check on Annie in a few minutes?" he asked Sara. When she agreed, he turned to Frank, "It's going to take me a couple hours to get into position. The way I remember it, that cabin is tucked into the hills on the far side of the lake." He looked to Jack for confirmation. "I'll park a couple miles away and hike in. I'll call when I get there. You guys can figure out a perimeter for surveillance. When Adam arrives, get him to set up on the northwest hill. We good?"

Frank met his eyes, and a slow grin lit his ugly chops. He lived for this kind of shit, they all did. It was in their blood, as necessary as breathing. Right there and then, Jared decided when they got the kids back, please Jesus safe and sound, he would ask his friends if they wanted to go into the security business with him. It would be almost like old times, just without the uniform.

"Watch your six. We'll be there as soon as we can." Frank murmured and slapped him on the back.

Nick let go of Sara long enough to come forward and clasp his hand. "Slow and easy, man."

"You're burning daylight, you going, or am I?" Jack's gruff voice made Jared smile. The fucker was growing on him.

"Watch your step, boys. I'll be setting up a little diversion once I get a positive ID." He strode for the door, stopping to gaze meaningfully at Jack. "Take care of her." The man nodded solemnly and Jared left, quick strides carrying him down the hall. He hesitated for a long moment at the women's restroom. He wished he could see her and make sure they were okay with one another before he left. Just in case. He shook off the bad feeling and hurried out to his truck.

Adam pulled into Tidal Falls at a little after two in the afternoon. He'd made good time from Seattle and was anxious to arrive at the sheriff's office and get an update on the Barnikov situation. The girl, Sandra, had turned out to be extremely helpful after she realized Maggie was one of the good guys. She'd explained how she'd been hurrying to work when a woman standing by the open hood of an older model sedan called out for help. Sandra knew better than to go near strangers, but the lady seemed like she was in genuine distress with her arms wrapped around a distended waist and tears streaming down her cheeks. Sandra asked what was wrong and the woman said she thought she was in labor and needed an ambulance. Sandra had looked down to find her phone in her purse and felt a sharp prick by the base of her neck. Confused and already fuzzy, she tried to talk but her tongue wouldn't work. Strong arms held her up and helped her into the back of the sedan. The woman climbed in beside her and yanked a pillow from under her shirt while the man slammed the hood down, hopped into the driver's seat and started the car. The woman twisted Sandra's face from side to side with cruel fingers; speaking in a language she didn't understand. Then everything went black.

She'd broken down for a while then, apologizing repeatedly to her parents for not listening to their advice. They wrapped comforting arms around their daughter and rocked back and forth, tears of anguish rolling down ravaged faces. Adam gave them time, his chest hurting over the lost innocence and trust. It would be a long journey for this family to function normally again, if they ever could.

When she calmed, Sandra described a room right out of a horror movie. Rows upon rows of thin army cots with many filled by naked chained women. When he asked, she answered yes, all nationalities. Most she figured around twenty to thirty years old, with her the youngest. The guards took pleasure taunting and teasing them. Adam asked the question he knew the parents needed answered. Had they molested her? They all sighed in relief when she said no, she hadn't been touched. He noticed her gaze dropped though, and her fingers pleated and un-pleated the sheet she kept tucked up around her chin. He silently cursed the fuckers straight to hell.

Sandra said she'd been there a couple of days when she noticed the black-haired woman. The guards would come, untie her in the morning and lead her from the room. When she returned, sometimes not until the next day, her skin would have marks on it and she'd look funny, sort of like Sandra had felt after the prick in the neck.

Adam's hands fisted so tight they turned white. The blood pounded in his head. They'd drugged her. No wonder Maggie wasn't able to get word out anymore. As to the marks; he couldn't think about that right now or he'd lose his freaking mind. Why had he ever agreed to her plan of going undercover to catch these guys in the first place? He was the senior partner, it was up to him to protect her and he'd failed. It didn't matter that he'd been against her going in from the start, he'd still allowed it. Now Maggie was paying the price. But not for much longer, he hoped.

As he wheeled into the sheriff's parking lot, Adam fingered the papers on the seat beside him. Sandra said she remembered the fake pregnant woman removing a brown wig, but that was all before she passed out so they had nothing more to go on there. But she'd done a bang-up job of describing the man who'd grabbed her and a sketch artist had been called in to get the details. Thanks to a brand new software program they'd managed to link the sketch to Sergei Barnikov, Russian Red Mafia, with known ties to the Mexican Sinaloa Cartel. The same organization they'd been chasing for the past three years. They'd long suspected the cartel of international ties. The capture of Sara's ex-husband last year and his subsequent confession had led them to Iraq and Adam's own brush with death. Now it seemed this was much more widespread than they'd realized. With the Russian connection they'd just opened a whole new can of worms. Besides drugs and money laundering, the Red Mafia liked to kidnap high-ranking diplomats or anyone of power, stage bank heists, and were actively involved in gunrunning, and human trafficking. If Mags were here, Adam would be celebrating. They'd just hit the mother-lode for career advancement. And it was all thanks to Maggie sacrificing herself to get the kid free with the info. She deserved a medal, and he was determined to make sure she was around to receive it. He needed Barnikov. Alive.

Adam climbed out of his rental, papers in hand, and made his way to the front door, squinting against the sun's glare on the glass. As soon as he entered, he wished himself outdoors again. The place was a madhouse, the front foyer filled to overflowing with chatting groups of people, some smiling, some clearly ticked off. He nosed his way through to the front counter and turned on the charm for the receptionist, whom he vaguely remembered from his last visit.

"Hi...Angel was it?" He folded his arms on the counter, hiding the papers out of view.

Angie smiled, tapped her cheek with a perfectly manicured red nail, and popped a wad of gum between matching colored lips. "Just because you're Irish, you don't need to be spreading the blarney everywhere you go, Agent O'Connor."

Adam smiled and shrugged. "Can't blame a guy for trying, can you?" He stood straight and nodded to the far door marked Sheriff's Office. "They in there?"

Angie moved to the side and lifted the countertop, allowing him to push his way through the swinging door below. "Yes, they're waiting on you. Ain't none too happy either," she said, then leaned close, sharing her spearmint-flavored breath. "Them poor kids."

Yeah, he couldn't have said it any better. He made his way through the bullpen, nodding at the officers eyeing him curiously, then gave a quick rap on the door before he pushed it open. Nick was the first to meet him on the other side. As his best friend pulled him into a tight clinch, Adam's eyes slid shut and his throat muscles worked overtime. He'd missed his buddy in the almost six years since the shooting in Iraq. So much water under the bridge. He hoped one day to receive the team's forgiveness, but he hadn't been given a choice.

Nick leaned back and looked him over. "You look like shit."

Adam barked out a rough laugh. "Thanks, man, missed you too." He slapped Nick's shoulder, then held on for a moment. "It's been a tough couple months."

"We heard." Adam turned at the chief's voice. A thousand complicated emotions rode a rollercoaster ride in his chest. This man had saved his life, more times than he could count. He idolized him. Yet now, because of Maggie, he resented him too.

"Frank, good to see you." He moved forward and clasped his old CO's baseball mitt-sized hand and shook, hard.

Frank coughed, his eyes mercury gray, and pointed to the papers. "You got something for us?" That was the chief, business first, everything else much, much later.

"I'm actually hoping we can help each other out." Adam turned toward the sheriff, nodded. "Sheriff Garrett, I wish I could say it's a pleasure. For a small town you manage to attract more than your share of criminals."

Jack sent a sarcastic glance at the other men, "I've noticed." He gave the map a slight twist and Adam focused on the triangulation marked out in red.

"This the search area?" he asked, taking a closer look. An oblong lake nestled amid fairly hilly territory. One road in and out, a major error on Barnikov's part. On the other hand, a cornered animal is a dangerous one. They'd have to plan this well, or the children could suffer the consequences.

"Yeah, we have a strong hunch," Jack said, and shrugged when Adam regarded him, brow raised in inquiry. "Jared Martin is on the way now to give it a combing over. We were just waiting for you before heading out ourselves."

Adam turned to Frank in disbelief. "You let him go in alone?" Fuck. When it came to those he cared about, Jared leaped first, and thought later. It had almost given him a one-way ticket to Shangri-La more than once. Even when Adam himself had been shot, it was Jared who'd jumped to his rescue, almost before he hit the ground. The guy had a death wish.

It was Nick who answered, his arm wrapped around his fiancé, Sara, who looked pale and uncertain. Belatedly, Adam recalled her daughter, Jessica, was one of the missing. "Come on, Adam, did you think we had a choice? It's his kid out there, of course he'd go."

Adam's mouth dropped open, this was news to him. No, he hadn't known Jared was a dad. Shit. This made an already complicated situation, a clusterfuck. Nothing he could do, the deed was done. The best he could hope for was that they could get out there before Jared blew Barnikov into a bazillion little pieces. Adam needed the Russian alive to tell him where to find Maggie.

"Well, what are we waiting for? Let's go."

CHAPTER TWENTY-TWO

Jared drove like a bat-out-o'-hell for the first couple of hours, then slowed to a crawl for the rough gravel road heading in to the lake. Now that he was getting close his nerves had steadied, though his hands were tense on the wheel. He knew and trusted his abilities, and those of his team following behind. But he was also aware he'd never played for more crucial stakes.

Jack was right to keep Annie in town where she'd be safe, but Jared hated the fact he hadn't had a chance to see her once more before he left. Just in case things went south. And those kind of thoughts were a good way to get himself killed. Keep his eyes on the endgame; his motto had kept him alive so far, let's hope it didn't fail him this time.

Focus shifting to the task at hand, Jared pulled to the side of the road and parked in a copse of thick bushes. His GPS told him he was still five miles from the lake. Good night for a run. He stepped out of the pickup and stilled, nose lifted to the sky as if he could scent his quarry. The evening was perfect for a hunt. Slight breeze, no more than four knots, and cloudy overhead, the better to hide his movements. He reached into the box behind his cab, grabbed his go-bag, threw it over his shoulder, and headed out cross-country. He planned to circle around behind and get a look at the lay of the land from the viewpoint of the hills at the far end of the lake. He hoped to end this quick; a few well-placed flash-bangs would give him an element of surprise.

His breathing slow and easy, Jared topped the rise just as the moon came out and cast its glow upon the lake below. Perfect timing. He dropped to his stomach and pulled the NVG's from his pack. Yep, just as he remembered, the cabin sat with its back facing him, squat against the hill he'd just climbed. A faint trail of smoke from the brick chimney proved someone was in residence, and he didn't think it was the Fowlers. He sent a quick text to Adam, their resident sniper. No answer. Not surprising out here, they'd been lucky to catch Barnikov's signal when it went out. He needed to get into a better position to see the front of the cabin. The only problem—it faced the lake. Jared's mouth twisted into a shark's smile. Ol' Sergei wouldn't be expecting anything in the water. Especially a SEAL.

He turned and made his way down the backside of the hill, grateful when the scudding clouds laid a thick blanket over the moon. Earlier, he'd set the bulk of his explosives close to the road. The plan—to make Barnikov think he was under siege should he try to escape. Jared worked his way around to the far side of the lake then carried the rest of the grenades with him down to the water's edge. He stripped down to his bvd's, all the while keeping a watchful eye on the cabin across the lake. He'd always been a water baby, but a mountain lake in the fall was bound to be its own form of Hell Week so he was glad he had his wetsuit in his pack.

One last fruitless try to send out a text to his team and Jared slid into the icy water with barely a ripple. He'd been right, it was fricken cold. NVG's in place, he power-stroked his way across the expanse, approximately a mile in width by his best guess. Fifty feet from shore he slowed, treading while he focused his goggles on the lone front window. The covered porch made it difficult to detect movement, but then a tall shadow blocked the flickering light coming from behind the curtained glass. Jared dropped down until his eyes were level with the surface of the lake. The last thing he wanted was to get caught out here with no cover.

Briefly he considered waiting until the rest of the team were in place, but anxiety was riding him hard. He needed to give Annie back her son. Their son. Knowing it was foolhardy, he lifted one hand clear of the dark water and threw the rock he'd carried with him toward the side of the cabin. It pinged off the step. The light inside snapped off. There was a sudden stillness to the very air. Then the door creaked open and a dark figure stepped out in a low crouch, leading with a gun. Either there were two criminals on the loose in the same general area, or Jared had just found his man.

Barnikov made his way carefully to the edge of the porch, the firearm balanced in one hand and braced by the other holding a flashlight. Jared let himself sink below the surface. He wasn't ready to announce himself just yet. At least he knew for sure where the prick had run. No sign of the kids though. He hoped they were tied up inside where they should be relatively safe. He held out for three minutes, then eased up. No sign of Sergei. Shit.

The door had closed, but that didn't tell him much. The Russian could be almost anyplace. He listened, but the slight breeze he'd been glad for earlier, now created ripples of sound everywhere. The waves slapping at the shoreline, fallen leaves skittering across the gravel drive, even the trees groaned their disapproval. Left with no choice, Jared swam to the wooden dock where he'd have some measure of protection. His intention was to draw the bastard away from the children so he could take him down, but first he had to locate him.

The light came back on inside the cabin. The door reopened. First Chris, then Jessica stepped into view. Relief that they seemed unharmed was quickly swamped by fury at the gun nudging their backs. Prick, Jared swore under his breath. This couldn't be good.

Chris's wobbly voice carried into the yard, "He says whoever you are, come out with your hands up, or he'll sho…shoot us."

Dammit. The poor kid was scared shitless. Jared was going to take extreme pleasure in beating the fuck out of the asshole when he caught him.

"No one's shooting anybody kid, just take it easy." He lifted his voice to carry across the yard. "I'm coming out, Barnikov." He heaved himself up onto the pier and slowly stood, hands out to the side. Awareness of the fact he was now a sitting duck had his heart threatening to erupt from his throat. Nothing like being made into a human target to get the old blood pumping. If it wasn't for the kids, he'd almost be having fun right now.

Reckless, foolhardy, adrenaline junkie, he'd heard them all at one time or another. And maybe it'd been true then, not so much anymore. Now he wanted a chance to watch his young son grow into a man. To wake up every morning with his body intertwined in mussed up sheets and sexy woman. He wanted to stand in the church, and watch Annie make her way down the aisle to join with him in holy matrimony. And he really wanted a chance to see her belly swell with another child, maybe a curly haired miniature of her this time. Hell, yeah.

Jared's pulse steadied, a calmness swept over him as he gazed up at the doorstep and the muzzle aimed at his chest. "Let the children go, Sergei. This is between you and me."

Barnikov growled from the darkness, "You don't learn very fast, Martin. You're not the one giving orders here, I am." He nudged Chris and Jessica forward with his free hand while keeping the weapon trained on Jared.

Jess gave a little yelp when her toe caught on the step. Chris glared over his shoulder, "Leave her alone, you big boogerhead."

That's my boy. Pride flared for the brave young man protecting his friend. But Jared didn't want Chris to give Sergei a reason to hurt him and opened his mouth to warn his son to keep quiet. A cry came from the far side of the cabin. His startled gaze went from the children to Annie, charging the porch like a diminutive Amazon

warrior. Sergei turned the gun toward the new
threat and Jared broke into a cold sweat, more
frightened than he'd ever been in his life.

Desperate to redirect the Russian's attention,
he pressed the button on the remote he'd
concealed in his outstretched hand. The perimeter
around the cabin exploded with smoke and noise
from the previously hidden flash-bangs. He
roared, lowering his arms to grab his Glock and
race for the end of the dock. Suddenly, what felt
like a mule kicked him in the chest and he
staggered, shocked at the pain. His hands
grasped at the burning sting, the impact of the
bullets sending him backward into the water.

Annie made her way in the dark, panting with
fear and exhaustion. She'd lost sight of Jared
almost immediately. There would be hell to pay
when he found out she'd hidden under a tarp in
the box of his truck. But there was no way she
was going to be left behind when the two most
important people in her world were in danger.
She followed the dirt road for what seemed like
hours. Every little creak and groan from the
shadowy forest placed her in heart attack
territory. An owl flew from the branches of a tree
in front of her. She screeched and ducked as it
swooped past with darkly gleaming eyes. Scared,
Annie broke into a run that lasted until she
smelled smoke. Slowing her pace, she scanned the
horizon, hoping the clouds would part enough to
show her the way. Then, she saw it, just the
faintest grey against the inky blackness of the
night. Picking her approach carefully now, she

made her way into the yard. There was a car parked beside an old wooden cabin. It was hard to tell in the dark, but it resembled the one Jared described as stolen.

Anxious and frightened, Annie rounded the corner of the house and froze. Just as in her dream, Jared stood on a wooden dock, arms raised in the air. A black wetsuit molded his powerful body. Goggles nestled in his moonshot hair. His attention was focused on the front porch of the cabin, and when she saw why, her mouth dropped opened in horror. Chris and Jessica were huddled on the stairs, held in place by a dark figure carrying a gun.

With only her child's safety in mind she charged, a mother bear protecting her cub. A banshee's screech erupted from her throat, drawing the man's gaze. His weapon swung toward her. Annie braced for the blast just as the ground shook with explosions that ripped the air apart. She fell to her knees, scarcely noticing the gravel digging into her palms. Dazed, she looked up in time to see Jared jerk backward and fall into the water, spray flying up around his body. Then she saw the smoking gun and screamed again. Panicked, she stumbled to her feet, desperation lending strength to her shaky legs, and ran towards the kids who had managed to break away when the explosions began. Annie swept them into her arms, ragged sobs tearing from her throat. The gunman jumped off the porch, and ignoring them, hurried for the dock, intent on checking the area for Jared.

Jared. God, she couldn't think about those bullets slamming into his body. He'd given his life to protect them. She couldn't let it be for nothing. Annie gathered the crying children close and hushed them. "Shh, it's okay. I need you to be strong for me now. We're going to wait until the bad man gets a little further away and then we're going to run as fast as we can for those trees over there, okay?"

Jessica looked up with tear-swollen eyes; great hiccupping sobs pushing their way out of her chest. "I want my mommy," she wailed.

"I know, honey, I know. Soon, okay? I promise." Annie squeezed the child's frail little shoulders. "Mommy and Nick want to see you too, they drove all night to get home so they could hug their girl."

"Why did that man take us away, Mom? He has a gun, did you see that?" Chris's green eyes glowed with a mixture of excitement and leftover fear. "Why did he shoot at Nick's friend? That's not very nice."

Annie choked back a sob of her own. "No, honey, that wasn't nice at all." She sliced a glance over her shoulder. No sign of Jared but the other man was almost to the dock. It was time to make their escape. She took a deep breath, exhaled, and forced a smile. "Okay, gang. We'll have a contest to see who can run the fastest. Ready?" They both nodded, their pale little faces scared but determined. "On the count of three. One...two...three!"

They took off, dust kicking up behind their flying heels. Annie took one last peek back, desperate to see Jared's head rising from the water. Then, heart pounding, she followed after the children, expecting to feel a bullet piercing her flesh with every step. They were almost to safety when a shout accompanied by a shell hitting the dirt a few feet between her and the kids had her slamming to a halt. Chris noticed her stopping and started to turn back.

"No," she screamed. "Go. Run, Chris. Take care of Jessica." Praying he'd listen, Annie turned and faced the enemy.

CHAPTER TWENTY-THREE

Jared came to, gasped, and drew in a lungful of icy water. He started to choke and automatically rolled to his side so he could spit the shit out. Fuck his chest hurt. For a moment he couldn't remember where he was or what had happened. His eyes opened, blinking away the dampness. He could see that he lay half under the dock, just at the water's edge. Good thing for the Kevlar or he would have more than just bruising to contend with.

The reverberations from the explosions was fading away, but the ringing in his ears made it hard to tell. He lifted his head enough to see up the shore. Annie. Where was she? Everything returned in an adrenaline rush. Jared's heart pounded, sending blood racing through his aching body. He bit back a harsh expletive and felt around for the gun. Nothing. *Shit.* Then he heard rocks skittering nearby and froze. Time was up.

He rotated the other way until he'd hidden in the shadow of the pier, most of his body under the water and held his breath. Heavy footfalls made the old wharf creak and groan beneath the man's weight. The silence, broken only by the splash of waves and the last of the flash-bangs going off in the distance and casting an eerie radiance over the scene, jangled his nerves. A scrape against the wood made his gaze narrow. In between the cracks he could see Sergei directly above him searching the water's edge. The flashlight's luminous glow edged closer. Jared's jaw tightened and his body readied, preparing for the inevitable detection.

The narrow path of light was no more than a foot away when it jerked up the hill toward the house. Sergei shouted something in Russian and fired a shot. Jared tried to get a look at what was happening and swore when he saw Annie turning, hands in the air, while the kids ran for the trees. Injuries forgotten, he surged up out of the water and grabbed Barnikov's ankle, pulling him off-balance. Sergei slammed to his back, shaking the dock. The satisfying splash of the gun hitting the drink put a wolf's smile on Jared's lips. They were even now. He took advantage of the moment and jumped onto the pier with a pained grunt, waiting in a half crouch for the other man to rise.

"C'mon, you pussy. Let's see what you can do when you're not protected by little kids." Rage enveloped him in a red haze as his mind filled with Chris's frightened little face. The tears rolling down Jessica's cheeks...and Annie, crazy, brave, impossibly beautiful Annie, standing in the face of danger if it meant saving her children.

Barnikov lifted his head from the dock, gave it a shake, then jumped up and lunged like a wounded animal. Jared, ready for him, came in low, wrapped his arms around the other man's thighs, and knocked them both off the wharf.

They hit the sand hard and rolled apart. Each rose cautiously to take the others' measure.

"You owe me redemption, Martin. You made me an embarrassment in front of my people." Sergei growled and shifted left, forcing Jared to the right, closer to the water's edge. "You must pay." He ducked on the last word and charged, catching Jared beneath his armpit with a meaty shoulder.

Jared grunted under the impact, and slammed his elbow into his assailant's neck, forcing him down and away. When Sergei came up he had a knife, the blade glinting wickedly under the light of the moon.

Annie screamed a warning. Caught off-guard, Jared glanced her way and paid the price with a slice across the rib section. The split-second glimpse had shown him that instead of running after the kids as he'd expected, she now stood no more than ten feet away, hands clasped to her throat in fear. For him.

"Annie, get back." Desperation lent strength to flagging muscles. He retrieved his Ka-bar from its sheath along his thigh and parried with a thrust of his own, forcing Sergei back and away. On a good day he might have stood a chance against the larger, more muscular Russian, but he was fairly certain the bullet had cracked or maybe even broken a rib. Breathing was a bitch, and every twist and turn to evade that steel blade was making things worse. He needed to take the big man down, once and for all.

They shuffled back and forth, arms extended in a macabre imitation of a waltz. Suddenly Sergei thrust forward. Jared feinted to the left and stuck out his foot, causing the other man to trip. But instead of hitting the ground he caught his balance and kept going, a bloodcurdling scream coming from his lips as he raised his knife and headed straight for a shocked Annie. Left with no option, Jared threw his Ka-bar. The knife buried itself between Sergei's shoulder blades with a sickening thud. His back arched with the impact and the scream turned to a gurgle, but still he kept moving, intent on a frozen Annie.

"Annie, for the love of God, run," Jared shouted, with the last of his strength before his knees gave out and he slumped to the sand. He watched in horror as Barnikov stumbled up the bank. Jared's words finally—too late—woke her to the danger. With a frightened gasp she backed up, eyes huge, and tripped over a log, falling on her ass in the sand.

Jared's heart threatening to erupt from his chest, he staggered to his feet, though he knew there was no chance of making it in time. Tears blurring his vision, he started forward then flinched at the report of a high-powered rifle shot.

Sergei dropped, dead before he hit the ground.

Ace, had to be. Adam was the sniper in their team. He rarely missed a shot, thank Christ. Jared hurried past; stopping only long enough to verify Barnikov was in fact finished. Yep, a shot between the eyes with a Remington is liable to do that to a person.

Annie lay where she'd fallen, her face porcelain white with shock, shamrock green eyes brimming with frightened tears. Alive. Relieved beyond words, Jared fell at her side and wrapped her tight in his arms, raining kisses everywhere he could reach. Annie shuddered and broke down, sobbing her heart out. He couldn't blame her, his own cheeks were still wet. He'd come so close to losing them tonight, the woman he'd always loved. His son.

Chris, where was he? Jared looked up in panic, only relaxing when he saw Frank, Nick, and Jack leading the children from the trees. Jessica had her head buried in Nick's neck as he held her close. Jared felt a flare of envy; he wanted to hug his child like that. Hopefully after they got to know each other Chris would give him a chance to be a father. Father. His chest filled with warmth. He leaned over and kissed Annie's trembling lips. His family.

Adam looked down on the trio in his scope, bitterness flooding his mouth. He'd had no choice. Barnikov wasn't going to be stopped by anything less than a kill shot, he'd seen it in the man's eyes. Revenge was a powerful motivator. In his years, first with the teams, then the DEA, Adam had witnessed the phenomena more than once; mortally wounded men, who somehow rose from deathbeds to land a last fatal blow before sliding into a hell of their own making.

He hadn't had a choice. But Maggie was going to pay for his decision. Angry, he dropped the rifle to his lap. He'd let her down, not just now, but all the times before also. From screwing around on her when they'd been a couple, to letting her accept the undercover gig in the first place. Oh sure, easy to say she'd trained for it, knew what she was getting into. It was a whole other thing to be the guy on the outside, waiting. Watching. Every time some John roughed her around, or a gangbanger tried to dope her up, Adam's tension wound tighter. He'd warned her time after time that he was going to go to the department head and get her pulled off the case, but she'd begged him to let her remain. Adam didn't know why, but he had a feeling this case was personal for her.

Then Maggie caught a break.

The Chinese-Mexican cartel lieutenant was known for his taste in prostitutes. Finally, her months of undercover work paid off, and Maggie was picked up. Adam rubbed a soft cotton cloth up and down the barrel of his gun. The DEA's mission was to find out about his money laundering, for that they needed someone on the inside. Maggie went in, she said, as Chenglei's housemaid, sending reports on a regular basis. But gradually the news slowed, and then stopped all together.

Frantic, Adam pressured his boss into getting a court order to search Chenglei's known residences, but of course he'd disappeared. The only thing they'd had to go on was Maggie's message about Barnikov and the Golden Key casino in Vegas. He dropped the cloth; eyelids squeezed closed and hands fisted at his side as his head fell back. He'd just executed the best shot he'd had at finding his partner.

Fuck.

He finished disassembling the gun, placed the pieces in the velvet-lined case, snapped the lid closed and strode off into the night.

Frank stood gazing down at the body of the Russian mobster and silently congratulated Adam on his shot. When they'd arrived in time for the light show, he'd sent his sniper up the hill, just in case. Nick and Jack worked their way to the east, while Frank took west, around back of the cabin. He'd seen Jared go down, and the ensuing fight after, but wasn't in the right position for a shot. Then the kids came bursting upon the scene and he'd had his hands full. Frank liked children, from a distance. There were little ones at the ranch, families of the men and women he employed, but he'd never had much to do with them. Since his brother disappeared, he'd closed himself off to everyone, except his mom and Jared.

He glanced over at the reunion going on a few feet away. Jared deserved some happiness in his life. Annie was perfect for him, spunky. She'd make him toe the line. Frank almost smiled. The boy looked just like him. Held his chin the same way and shared the same nose. They would make a good family.

Nick too, Sara's little girl hadn't let go of him since they arrived. Her eyes fairly glowed with love for her soon-to-be-stepdad. And he wore such a sappy look on his face it was almost embarrassing to see. Frank knew Nick had issues after some of his teammates died and he'd been injured. It had taken some time but he was on the road to recovery now with plenty of loving support.

That left him and Adam. Magdalena Holt popped into his head, not that she was ever far away from his thoughts. Funny how a woman he barely knew could occupy such a large part of his mind. Problem was, she wasn't his to think about. It was obvious when he'd seen her and Adam together in Tidal Falls last spring, that the two of them had history. Frank wasn't getting into the middle of that, no matter how much the woman fascinated him.

Shaking his head over his whimsies, Frank hunted for Jack, who was over checking the ground near the wharf—probably for the missing guns—before he bent over the body to do a quick search before the feds took over. Call him crazy but he liked to cross his T's and dot his I's. Deep in the man's front pocket, Frank found a photo. He pulled it out to have a quick scan, and then froze in the act of folding it over. It was a picture of Maggie. She laid asleep, her raven's wing hair fanned out across a snowy white pillow. The sheet lay across her pelvis, showcasing her naked body. Frank skimmed past dusky nipples back to her face. Something wasn't right. And then he saw it. Her wrists were handcuffed to the headboard.

What the fuck?

He knew she'd gone undercover as a prostitute. She'd been dressed as one the day they met when he went to pick up Jared from the LVPD. But this was something else. Frank couldn't see her willingly going through with actual intercourse, much less something like this. And what the hell did Barnikov have to do with it? He needed to talk to Adam, ASAP.

He stepped away from the others and made the call.

"Yeah?" Adam's voice came through disgruntled, angry.

"Good shot," Frank said, and then decided to skip the niceties, "where's your partner?"

There was a long tension-filled pause, then Adam released a loud sigh. "I don't know. She's missing."

Just what he'd been afraid of. "I've got info." He was already on the move. "You show me yours, I'll show mine." Nick and Jack had each brought out their own vehicles so he wasn't worried about leaving them. He could get hold of Jack later. He knew the other man would need a statement from him.

"Oh and by the way...I want in."

EPILOGUE

Annie shuffled the morning papers around on the coffee shop's back table, and stopped to have a sip of her coffee. Lifting the mug, she inhaled the dark roast aroma and eyed the room, tapping her toe to the dance tune coming from the jukebox. Mr. Abraham sat chatting with Betty-Lou a couple of booths away. Good to see they'd settled their differences, for a while anyway. Jack and his Aunt Tess were behind them, eating apple pie and ice cream by the look of it. He lifted the fork to his mouth, caught her eye, and smiled. They were going to be okay. Annie was glad; she genuinely cared for him and would have hated to lose their friendship. Grace and Susan stood at the till, gossiping with Rebecca's mom, Angie.

Just then the door jingled and in raced her reason for living. Chris ran down the aisle, and not far behind him a smiling, relaxed Jared.

"Mom, guess what? Jared took me fishing, and we caught a *big* one." He skidded to a stop beside her, his hands stretching wide to show her the size.

"Wow, son, that is a big one." Annie's lips twitched at the expanse. He was already learning to tell tall-tales, it seems. She opened her arms for a hug and he jumped in, full of youthful exuberance. He smelled of the outdoors, mud, fresh air, and little boy. Her throat closed up with love, and he groaned when her arms tightened their grasp.

"Mom, you're squishing me, let go." He wriggled free just as Jared reached the table. He glanced quizzically at the papers, and then smiled at her. Annie's heart jumped at the warmth and promise radiating from his eyes.

He placed a gentle hand on his son's head and turned him toward his grandmother. "Why don't you go see if your grandma made any cookies today, partner?"

"Woohoo, cookies. Can I, Mom?" Big green eyes, so much like his father's, pleaded with her to break the no-snacks-before-dinner rule.

"Okay, but only one. You need to eat supper if you're going to be a fisherman." He was gone almost before she agreed. She watched him run to Jared's mom, who scooped him up with a laugh and peck on the cheek. Now that she could acknowledge her grandson publicly—Grace had stated to Annie she'd known all along—she seemed to have a new lease on life. Her cheeks were a healthy pink, and her diabetes readings were in the normal range. Good news for all of them, but especially Jared who'd confided his fear of her health to Annie.

Now that their son was occupied, Jared moved, leaning down to give her a tender kiss. "Hi."

She smiled and wrapped her arms around his neck. "Hi, back. I missed you."

Those perfect lips inched closer until they barely touched hers. "How much?" The words feathered against her mouth, and her pulse tumbled like an acrobat on the high wire. Annie couldn't resist. Her tongue slipped out and teased him back. He tasted like sunshine, meadows, and man, and she loved him more than life. Her grip on his neck tightened when he growled and took the kiss deeper, wetter, hotter.

The clapping and cheering finally broke through the haze and they slowed the tempo. Jared gave her one last lingering kiss before moving away, a soft glow turning his eyes ethereal.

"I love you, Jared Mathew Martin," she whispered, her cheeks warm now that she realized they had an audience.

Jared ignored the crowd, his gaze focused solely on her. "I love you, Annie Campbell. I always have, and I always will." His expression turned fierce. "You and Chris are everything to me. If anything had happened..."

Annie's heart kicked over. She knew how he felt. It petrified her to think of him getting shot, not knowing if he were alive or dead, while a mad man held her son. Thank God it was over now, and other than badly bruised ribs, Jared had escaped serious injury.

"Dad, look what I have." Chris's words had the effect of a rainbow on a cloudy day. The adults around him froze a startled moment. Annie looked at the shocked wonder on Jared's face and her eyes teared up with happiness for him.

They were all going to be just fine.

SIGN UP TO MY NEWSLETTER HERE

Subscribe to My mailing list to find out first about upcoming releases, contests, recipes, and more.
www.jacquiebiggar.com,
or
Paste this into your URL
http://eepurl.com/2MFvX

Thank you for taking time to read The Rebel's Redemption. If you enjoyed it, please consider telling your friends or posting a short review. Word of mouth is an author's best friend and much appreciated.

Links to my website and social media where I talk about H O T guys and dogs are below:

http://jacquiebiggar.com
http://Facebook.com/jacqbiggar
http://Twitter.com/jacqbiggar

ABOUT THE AUTHOR

From the time I was twelve years old, I knew I wanted to be a writer. That year I wrote a short story called Count Daffodil for my English Assignment. It garnered me an A and was read aloud through the school's loudspeaker system. Needless to say, after that I was hooked.

I grew up, got married, raised a family and left my writing urges to simmer in the background unattended.

I owned and operated a successful diner in my hometown for a number of wonderful years. Now I'm ready to take up the writing reins and see how far I can travel.

I expect it to be an exciting, new journey and would be honored to have your company along the way.

http://jacquiebiggar.com
http://Facebook.com/jacqbiggar
http://Twitter.com/jacqbiggar